"I don't ever want to hurt you," he said.
"Or take advantage of you in any way."

Fiona knew that if she let Greg walk out of her life without having experienced his lovemaking, she would regret it for the rest of her life. She wanted no regrets. Not where Greg was concerned.

With a calm deliberation, Fiona stood and briskly peeled off her clothes. Greg, startled, sat up and said, "What are you doing?"

Of course he knew what she was doing, she thought, as she sat beside him once more. His gaze seemed to sweep over her in waves, and everywhere his gaze paused, she tingled.

"I'm seducing you," she said, sounding breathless as she slid her arms around his neck and kissed him.

Dear Reader,

As you ski into the holiday season, be sure to pick up the latest batch of Silhouette Special Edition romances. Featured this month is Annette Broadrick's latest miniseries, SECRET SISTERS, about family found after years of separation. The first book in this series is *Man in the Mist* (#1576), which Annette describes as "...definitely a challenge to write." About her main characters, Annette says, "Greg, the wounded lion hero—you know the type— gave me and the heroine a very hard time. But we refused to be intimidated and, well, you'll see what happened!"

You'll adore this month's READERS' RING pick, *A Little Bit Pregnant* (SE#1573), which is an emotional best-friends-turned-lovers tale by reader favorite Susan Mallery. *Her Montana Millionaire* (SE#1574) by Crystal Green is part of the popular series MONTANA MAVERICKS: THE KINGSLEYS. Here, a beautiful socialite dazzles the socks off a dashing single dad, but gets her own lesson in love. Nikki Benjamin brings us the exciting conclusion of the baby-focused miniseries MANHATTAN MULTIPLES, with *Prince of the City* (SE#1575). Two willful individuals, who were lovers in the past, have become bitter enemies. Will they find their way back to each other?

Peggy Webb tantalizes our romantic taste buds with *The Christmas Feast* (SE#1577), in which a young woman returns home for Christmas, but doesn't bargain on meeting a man who steals her heart. And don't miss *A Mother's Reflection* (SE#1578), Elissa Ambrose's powerful tale of finding long-lost family...and true love.

These six stories will enrich your hearts and add some spice to your holiday season. Next month, stay tuned for more page-turning and provocative romances from Silhouette Special Edition.

Happy reading!

Gail Chasan
Senior Editor

Please address questions and book requests to:
Silhouette Reader Service
U.S.: 3010 Walden Ave., P.O. Box 1325, Buffalo, NY 14269
Canadian: P.O. Box 609, Fort Erie, Ont. L2A 5X3

Man in the Mist

ANNETTE BROADRICK

Silhouette®

SPECIAL EDITION™

Published by Silhouette Books

America's Publisher of Contemporary Romance

This book is dedicated to

Eileen Hutton—
A keen mind
and gentle heart...
a winning combination

 SILHOUETTE BOOKS

ISBN 0-373-24576-9

MAN IN THE MIST

This edition published by arrangement with Harlequin Books S.A.

® and TM are trademarks of Harlequin Books S.A., used under license. Trademarks indicated with ® are registered in the United States Patent and Trademark Office, the Canadian Trade Marks Office and in other countries.

Visit Silhouette at www.eHarlequin.com

Printed in U.S.A.

ANNETTE BROADRICK

believes in romance and the magic of life. Since 1984, Annette has shared her view of life and love with readers. In addition to being nominated by *Romantic Times* as one of the Best New Authors of that year, she has also won the *Romantic Times* Reviewers' Choice Award for Best in its Series; the *Romantic Times* WISH award; and the *Romantic Times* Lifetime Achievement Awards for Series Romance and Series Romantic Fantasy.

Glen Cairn

SCOTLAND

Craigmor

Stirling

Glasgow   Edinburgh

IRELAND

ENGLAND

All underlined places
are fictitious.

Prologue

November 28, 1978

"I know, I know," Dr. James MacDonald murmured. "The contractions are coming harder and with more pain," he said to the girl who lay on the table in one of his examining rooms. "You're doing fine…just fine."

She'd shown up at his home office earlier that evening, chilled from the cold wind sweeping across the Highlands of Scotland. He had never seen her before but when he realized she was having contractions, he never thought about turning her way, despite the late hour.

His wife, Margaret, stood near the girl's head and wiped away the perspiration from her face and forehead. "Everything's going well," Margaret said to her, but the look on her face told James she was worried.

The girl was running a high fever. He'd done what he could to give her medications that wouldn't distress the babies he was in the process of delivering. She needed to be in a hospital, but he couldn't move her until the babies were born.

Triplets, she'd told him.

He looked at her now as she rested between contractions. "What is your name, dear?" he asked.

"Moira," she replied.

"Ah, Moira. And where is your husband on this blustery night?"

Moira shook her head and began to cry. "He's dead," she sobbed. "I saw his brother kill him and I ran. I had to get away before he killed me, as well." Her voice climbed.

"Well, you needn't worry about a thing, dear. You're safe with Meggie and me." After a moment he asked, "What was your husband's name?"

"Douglas, but please don't put his name on the birth certificates. If you do, his brother will find us."

"Don't you worry, lass. You're safe and so are your babes. Rest as much as you can. I believe these babes are eager to enter the world."

"They're a little early," she said. "My doctor told me he would place me in hospital for the last two weeks. Our plans were to go in next week." She gasped as another strong contraction began.

James MacDonald had practiced medicine in his hometown of Craigmor for more than thirty years and had dealt with a great many crises. Tonight he was facing a particularly difficult one. His young patient, and he doubted she was more than eighteen or so, was fighting a severe lung infection in addition to having her babies.

After several hours of labor, three tiny but healthy girls entered the world. Each had strong vocal cords and wasn't afraid to use them. Margaret cleaned and weighed each one before wrapping them in warm blankets. Then, she tucked them side by side in a bassinet.

"Mighty fine young ladies you have, Moira," James said, feeling relief that they were safely delivered. "All of them beauties, just like their mother."

The new mother attempted a smile before she closed her eyes. Her work was done. Her babies had made it safely into the world.

James moved her into one of their upstairs bedrooms to rest and recuperate while Margaret continued to care for the infants.

Before she fell asleep, Moira caught James's wrist in a surprisingly fierce grip, considering her weakened condition, and said, "Don't let him find my babies.'' Her eyes were glazed with fever and her voice sounded raspy. ''He mustn't find them. He'll kill them. Please. Don't let him find them.''

''You and your babies are safe, Moira. You just rest and get better. You'll be able to take care of them yourself once you're better.''

Moira stared at him, her grief and pain mirrored in her eyes. ''I loved Douglas so much. I don't want to go on without him,'' she whispered.

''You have three precious daughters to care for, Moira,'' he replied in a gentle voice. ''They need you.''

''Please find them a good home. Promise me,'' she whispered. ''Promise me you'll protect my babies.''

James stared at her in alarm. ''*You* must protect your babies. Give yourself time. You will be able to…'' He stopped speaking when he realized she was no longer conscious.

Moira never regained consciousness. It was as though she'd grown tired of struggling for breath and at the end gave up the effort with one final sigh.

Moira with no last name had done what she could to give her babies a chance at life. Now it was up to James and Margaret to decide what to do with her legacy.

Chapter One

October 16, 2003

Greg Dumas peered through the windshield of his rental car with a mixture of frustration and resignation. He could scarcely see past the front of his car. He leaned closer while the windshield wipers valiantly fought a losing battle to remove moisture from the fogged glass. Rain poured down, mixing with the heavy mist that swirled in the headlights.

After several weeks in Scotland, he felt as though he'd stepped into another world made up of perennial rain and perpetual gloom.

Greg knew he should have stayed in Craigmor tonight, rather than attempt to find one small village in the western Highlands after dark. The village hadn't looked so far away on the map, but he hadn't taken into account that he was in the mountains.

He was exhausted. It didn't help that the cough that had started sometime last week had worsened. He'd been on the move since landing in Glasgow last month. He'd rented a car and driven to Edinburgh, thinking he'd be returning to New York in no more than three days. Instead, Edinburgh had been the first stop of many in his search. Since then, he'd followed one lead after another, chasing back and forth across the Highlands like a deranged bloodhound.

When he'd received the newest lead late this afternoon, he hadn't wanted to wait another night to check it out.

Greg knew he sounded like a barking seal every time he coughed. In addition, his head felt stuffed full of cotton and he couldn't breathe without wheezing.

To make matters worse, it was now close to midnight and he was lost. He thought he'd been following the map he'd marked earlier when he stopped to eat, but somehow he'd managed to find yet another narrow road that appeared to lead to nowhere.

He couldn't remember the last light he'd seen.

Of course, with fog so thick, he could have driven through the hamlet—or the village, or whatever the towns were called—without being aware he'd reached his goal.

Manhattan was nothing like this, he muttered to himself.

He should never have taken this job, he thought—not for the first time—regardless of the money offered. In the three years since he'd opened his office as a private investigator, what had started as a one-man operation had mushroomed into a firm with several investigators—former cops as he was—and a growing support staff that threatened to spill out of their office space within the year.

So why had he finally agreed to take this case? It hadn't been the money, although the client had offered to double his usual fee and pay all of his expenses if he would personally handle this matter.

He'd turned her down at first. He'd never been away from his daughter, Tina, for more than a night and he hadn't been comfortable with the idea of traveling to Great Britain. However, Tina's grandmother, Helen, had urged him to take the case. She'd felt he needed a change of pace from his busy schedule as well as a chance to see more of the world.

When Helen convinced him that leaving Tina with her would be fun for all concerned, he'd finally accepted the assignment. Of course, he'd taken this job thinking he'd quickly find the answers he sought.

Instead he was chasing false trails or trails that dried up, leaving him wondering where to search next, all because he respected Helen's opinion.

He didn't know what he would have done if his mother-in-law hadn't stepped in and helped him to take care of Tina after Jill's death. She rarely offered her opinion. When she did, he listened.

After three weeks in Scotland, he had no doubts that he'd made the wrong choice. What he had thought would be a simple matter—finding his client's birth parents—had turned out to be far from simple. His search had turned into a mystery with few answers.

If this latest lead didn't pan out, he would give up and return to New York. He'd exhausted all other avenues.

Right now, all he wanted to do was to hop on a plane and head for the States, sleeping the entire trip across the Atlantic. Unfortunately, that wasn't going to happen. Instead, he appeared destined to wander the western Highlands of Scotland for the foreseeable future.

Greg knew he'd been on the road too long and had driven too many hours. He had to find a place where he could rest, and soon. Better yet, he needed to find a place to spend the night. Between the cold air and the dampness that had seeped inside him clear to his bones, he seemed to have acquired a permanent tremor throughout his body.

His assignment had turned into a wild-goose chase. Unfortunately for him, he didn't have the protective coating of a wild goose. The cold, damp climate had him reeling.

He'd headed west to find some middle-aged woman who had retreated to the isolated area of northwest Scotland. She'd been nowhere near the village where he had hoped to find the information he needed.

From his interviews with several of the old-time residents of Craigmor, this particular woman was his best hope to discover the answers he needed.

When he first arrived in Scotland he'd expected to contact the attorney who had handled his client's adoption and/or the physician attending her birth to get the name of her biological parents.

The first snag he'd run into involved making contact with the lawyer, Calvin McCloskey. Greg had gone to the address listed in the legal documents. There were still lawyers at the location—they called themselves solicitors—and the name of the firm was the same, but as the associate he'd spoken to pointed out, the adoption papers had been signed twenty-five years ago. The solicitors who'd been practicing law back then had all retired or died.

Greg had had a moment of concern that Mr. McCloskey was one of the guys who'd died, but the associate assured him that good ol' Calvin was still alive and kicking. In fact, the associate had given Greg Calvin's home address and wished him well.

Fat lot of good that had done him. He'd talked to the man's housekeeper, who explained that Mr. McCloskey was off fishing. Since he hadn't bothered telling her where he would be, Greg had no way of contacting him until he decided to return home.

Greg had had the choice of waiting for the man or searching for the doctor. But he could find no record of a Dr. MacDonald currently practicing in Edinburgh.

He'd had to wait for the solicitor.

Greg had passed the time while waiting for Mr. McCloskey by visiting several Edinburgh sights. He'd been impressed to see how well maintained the castles were and had enjoyed catching up on the history of the area.

By the end of the first week he'd adjusted to the Scottish brogue that he heard everywhere he went. In addition, he'd managed to stop going to the left side of the rental car to drive, since the steering wheel could only be found on the right side.

Late the following week Mr. McCloskey left word at Greg's hotel that he could meet with him the following day.

They had the meeting at the solicitor's home. The man was gracious enough but for Greg's purposes frustratingly reserved. As soon as Greg explained why he was there, the man's air of detached interest disappeared and he stated firmly that he wouldn't be able to help him.

He gave various excuses, among them that his files were in storage and he would have no idea where to find one particular file.

Greg could understand that after twenty-five years, finding one lone file would be difficult. However, he found the solicitor's manner a little strange when Mr. McCloskey began to question Greg about his client, wanting to know her name and something about her.

After explaining that he couldn't ethically give information about his client's present situation, Greg showed him the birth certificate and adoption papers he'd brought with him and pointed out that the birth parents were not listed. He'd found that unusual and hoped the solicitor could shed some light on the mystery.

Calvin sighed and leaned back into his chair. He stroked his chin and gazed pensively out a nearby window. Finally, he turned and said, "Nothing good is going to come out of this search of yours. Why don't you go back to New York and tell your client that her parents were the ones who provided her a loving home."

Greg leaned forward. "You talk as if you knew her adoptive parents."

"That I did, young man. A fine, upstanding couple."

"In that case, you must know the birth parents. How else would you have known my client was a candidate for adoption?"

Mr. McCloskey folded his hands and shook his head. "I was asked to handle the matter by the doctor who delivered the—uh—who delivered your client," he muttered.

"Dr. MacDonald," Greg replied. "Do you know how I could contact him?"

"I doubt you'll get much from him...or his wife, for that matter...seeing as how they're both buried in a cemetery near Craigmor."

Greg felt his heart sink. "Dr. MacDonald is dead?"

"Aye. It was a heartbreaking day when I heard about his and Meggie's sudden passing," McCloskey said sadly, shaking his head.

The solicitor showed the first emotion Greg had seen since he'd arrived. Intrigued, Greg asked, "What happened to them?"

McCloskey's eyes misted over. "Jamie and I had been school chums who had kept in touch with each other through the years. I expect I knew him as well as anyone. I for one was not in the least surprised to hear that Jamie and Meggie died helping to save others." He stared into space. "They'd gone to Ireland to visit with friends, I was told. On the way home, the ferry they were on malfunctioned—no one knows exactly why—and sank.

"Survivors told me how heroic Jamie had been,

refusing to leave the ferry until every person was safely aboard the lifeboats. Of course Meggie would be right beside him, as she was most of their lives.

"One woman told me how she would have lost her two children if the MacDonalds hadn't scooped them up and placed them into one of the boats. The children's mother begged the MacDonalds to get in the boat with them, but neither would listen, saying there were others to be helped. The last she saw of them, they'd returned to the main deck. The ferry sank quickly after that.

"By the time help found them, there was nothing to be done. The only consoling thing that came out of the tragedy was that the two of them went together. I doubt that either of them would have survived long without the other."

Greg allowed the silence to stretch into minutes. Mr. McCloskey was obviously back in the past, reliving the days when all of them had been young.

Finally, Greg said, "You know, Mr. McCloskey, Dr. MacDonald sounds like the kind of person who would want a girl to know who her birth parents were. Tell me, did he practice here in Edinburgh?"

"No. He returned to Craigmor, his hometown, when he finished school. He practiced medicine there for years as the only medical resource for miles around."

Craigmor. That gave him a lead of sorts. Not much, but enough to visit the place to see if anyone living there now might remember that time and offer some answers.

Greg had decided that he wasn't going to receive anything more from the solicitor when Mr. McCloskey suddenly spoke, as though to an unseen person nearby. "It's been almost twenty-five years now, Jamie. Haven't we protected the wee babes long enough? Maybe it's time they found each other."

Greg knew he must have heard the man wrong. Did he say babes? "There was more than one?" he asked softly, not wanting to startle the solicitor from his reverie. Greg's heart had started to pound with the excitement of discovering an unexpected aspect of the case.

Mr. McCloskey slowly nodded, then took off his wire-rimmed glasses and carefully polished them with a snowy white handkerchief. He took his time before carefully folding the handkerchief and returning it to his pocket.

"There were triplets," he finally said. "It was a terrible time. We had to make one of the most difficult decisions possible—we knew the most important thing was to find the girls suitable homes away from the area as quickly as possible."

"Which is why you split them up." Greg's comment was more statement than question.

Calvin nodded. "Yes. We needed to protect them from harm."

"Why would they need to be protected?" Greg asked, his curiosity fully aroused.

"I was told that their father had been murdered by his brother the night before their birth and the mother had run away, seeking sanctuary. By the time she appeared in Craigmor, she suffered from a combination of shock, grief and pneumonia and died soon after delivering the babies. She'd been terrified their uncle would find the girls and kill them. She begged the MacDonalds to protect them."

Greg thanked the saints for Mr. McCloskey's willingness, at long last, to share information with him. "Did you learn the parents' names at the time of the adoption?"

"No, none of us did. The mother—Moira was her name—never gave her last name. Moira mentioned her husband, Douglas. Not only did the MacDonalds never find out the mother's last name, they had no idea where she had come from. For obvious reasons they were hesitant to make too many inquiries for fear of stirring up too much interest from the wrong source."

Greg took notes furiously, wondering how he should tell his client. She was one of three. That news was going to be a shock.

"Jamie and Meggie went to a great deal of effort to protect the girls from being found by their uncle," the solicitor continued sadly.

Greg stood and held out his hand. "Thank you

for being so candid with me, sir. I have to admit I now have more questions than answers, but I believe you've guided me to the next step.''

Mr. McCloskey also stood, shaking Greg's hand. ''Which is?'' he asked, frowning.

''I'd like to find any relatives of the Mac-Donalds to see if they recall that time.'' He looked at his notes. ''You mentioned Craigmor, I believe. I'll continue my search there.''

Mr. McCloskey adjusted his glasses. ''I doubt very much that you'll find any answers there.'' He sounded irritated, as though he'd hoped Greg would give up looking for more information.

''Probably not, but as long as I'm here in Scotland, I need to exhaust all leads before returning home,'' Greg had replied at the time.

The solicitor had certainly been correct, Greg thought now as he strained to see the road ahead. Greg had never found such a closemouthed bunch of people before, which was saying a lot. Every villager he'd gotten to talk with him had been adamant that no triplets had ever been born in their village.

How could that be? he'd wondered. Had Mr. McCloskey made up the whole story to get rid of him? Greg found that hard to believe. The crusty solicitor had been too reticent at first to discuss the matter to have decided to make up a lie. If Greg were any judge of character, he'd swear the man had told the truth.

So when one of the old-timers happened to mention the MacDonalds' daughter, Greg decided he would search her out before reporting his findings to his client. He wished he'd forgotten about following this lead and had returned home, instead. He could have told his client there wasn't a chance of finding her roots in Scotland.

However, in good conscience, Greg couldn't do that because there *was* a chance, even though it was slight. Perhaps the daughter, Fiona MacDonald, would remember something that would open up his search. If she couldn't? Well, so be it. Until he had a chance to talk with her, she was a lead he refused to ignore.

Another wracking cough took over his body and forced Greg once more to slow the car. At least he didn't have to worry about someone coming along and rear-ending him before he or she saw him through the fog.

No intelligent being would be out on a night like this, which said a great deal about him, he thought sourly.

Some time later Greg knew he was hallucinating when he thought the mist formed into wings and a long wisp pointed to the right. Another ten feet and he spotted a small lane, smaller than the one he was on. Despite the poor visibility, Greg could see that the road appeared to lead to a higher elevation. There was no sign to tell him where it led, but he had the strongest urge to follow it. Maybe he would find a farmhouse where he could get directions to the nearest town.

Without questioning the wisdom of his decision, Greg turned in to the single-track lane. A stone fence on either side of the road made him wonder what a person would do if he were to meet another vehicle along the way. There was no room to pass or turn around. He supposed if he met someone, one of them would have to back up. From the lack of lights or directional signs, he had a hunch he wouldn't have to worry about that particular problem this late at night.

Fiona MacDonald sat beside the fireplace of her snug cottage, curled up with the latest novel by one of her favorite authors. Engrossed in the imaginary world portrayed in its pages, she'd lost track of time. A warm, knitted afghan on her lap had become a bed for Tiger, her striped yellow cat, who was sprawled on his back with paws extended in the air, asleep in total bliss.

Next to the chair, her mastiff, McTavish, soaked up the warmth radiating from the peat fire.

Fiona had spent most of the day visiting several villagers in the glen who'd needed her services as a healer. Once she'd returned home she'd been physically tired, but not ready for sleep. Rather than go upstairs to bed, she'd decided to indulge herself in her favorite pastime—reading—before retiring.

Although she heard nothing more than the sounds of the fire and the soft snores emanating from Tiger, McTavish lifted his head and stared toward the front window. Fiona put down her book and listened. She still heard nothing. Mac's hearing was almost supernatural, so she waited to detect the sound that he had heard.

Eventually, a weak light appeared, barely piercing the thick fog, and Fiona realized someone was driving up her lane. She sighed and reluctantly moved Tiger off her lap. She glanced at her watch. It was past midnight. If there was an emergency, why hadn't someone phoned her instead of driving out here in such weather at this time of night?

Thankful she still wore her heavy sweater and woolen pants instead of her nightgown and robe, Fiona slipped her stocking feet into her shoes and went to the front door, McTavish by her side. She grabbed her heavy jacket from the coat tree beside the door and pulled it on, making sure the hood came snugly over her head. Only when she opened the door did she realize that the earlier rain she'd been absently hearing had turned into stinging pellets of sleet.

She and McTavish stepped outside and stood in the shelter of her porch waiting for the car—which crept forward—to reach the house. McTavish had not barked as yet. However, his alert stance would make it clear to anyone venturing near his mistress that if he perceived her to be in danger, he was ferociously prepared to fend off any would-be attacker.

The car inched into the yard and stopped near the garage, which was unattached to the house. Fiona turned on the yard light, thinking she might recognize her late-night visitor. Whoever was in the car left the headlights on and she couldn't see inside.

She watched as a man wearing a jacket inadequate for the current weather conditions stepped out of the car. He stood with the door open and looked around the area, pulling his collar up around his ears. Mist floated between them and the sleet further obscured him from view.

McTavish rumbled deep in his chest, but didn't move. She rested her hand lightly on his head. The man spotted her in the shadows and without moving away from the car spoke to her.

"I'm sorry to bother you so late," he said with an American accent, his voice hoarse, "but I'm afraid I'm lost." He began to cough—a horrible, deep paroxysm that must have been painful. "I was hoping for some directions to a town nearby where I might find a place to stay overnight."

Fiona knew that her visitor—whoever he was—was ill. She could never turn away someone in need of healing.

She stepped forward so that he could better see her and spoke clearly so that he might hear her. "Come in, please. You don't sound at all well."

He shook his head. ''No, but thanks. I'm all right. I just need some directions.''

The yard light shone down on his thick, dark hair and emphasized his high cheekbones and a strong jaw that reflected the stubbornness she could hear in his voice.

Fiona stared at him without speaking, a tingle of sensation reverberating through her body. She began to receive myriad sensations about this man—a long-harbored and deep grief…depleted energy…frustration… physical pain. Most immediate to her, though, was the instinctive knowledge that he was on the verge of pneumonia.

At least he'd come to the right place for healing. He probably didn't know he'd found a medical person, of sorts. Well, tonight was his lucky night, she thought with wry humor.

''Please come inside and we'll discuss your situation,'' she said. ''You need to get out of this weather.''

He glanced around as though only now aware of the sleet stinging his face. With a shrug of resignation, the man reached inside the car, turned off the engine and lights and slammed the door behind him.

He strode across the driveway toward the front door.

As soon as he stepped onto the porch, she opened the door and motioned for him to enter. Now that she was closer to him, Fiona knew her sensory impressions had been correct. Her unexpected visitor was far from well. She felt certain he had a fever. That, together with his croupy cough, informed her that if he didn't already have pneumonia, he was close to succumbing.

McTavish followed her visitor into the house, staying between the stranger and Fiona, totally focused on the man who had entered their home. Fiona smiled to see how seriously McTavish took his role as her protector whenever a stranger appeared. She rarely had visitors whom she didn't know. She found this one to be particularly intriguing, whether from a healer's point of view or as a woman aware of a very attractive man, she wasn't certain.

However, she intended to find out. She closed the door behind them and moved toward him with a smile.

Greg looked around the hallway, then back to her as though bewildered. She held out her hand. "I'm Fiona MacDonald…and you are…?"

He blinked. "You're Fiona MacDonald? I don't believe it! You're the woman I've been looking for. I'm Greg Dumas," he said, and shook her hand.

The contact shook her. Or maybe her reaction was due to his comment.

She was the woman he'd been looking for, was she? Quite a startling revelation, if he were to be believed. Had he had the same reaction to her as she had to him?

Somehow she doubted it. Her own true love arriving at midnight on a stormy night proclaiming—with an American accent!—that he had been searching for her and at last had found her was a little much, even for her romantic soul.

His stare tended to unnerve her. If he hadn't known her before, he would certainly know her after this, she decided, slipping out of her heavy jacket.

She gestured to the living room. "You're chilled, which is to be expected with the weather as it is. Your jacket isn't much protection on a night such as this one. Please warm yourself by the fire. I'll be right back with some tea to help ease your throat."

He stared at her blankly and she wondered if he had understood her. He closed his eyes tightly, then opened them, blearily focusing on her.

After a pause, he replied, "Oh, that's okay," as though her words had finally registered. "I can't stay." He swayed where he stood. "What I really need are directions."

Oh, my. He was going to be very stubborn about this. She'd certainly read that jawline correctly. He was operating on sheer willpower alone. He blinked his eyes again, as though trying to improve his vision. When he saw her watching him, he smiled uncomfortably. She found his lopsided smile endearing. He was exhausted and refused to admit it.

She nodded toward the front room. ''I won't be long,'' she said, showing that she could be just as stubborn. ''Go ahead and get warm, now.'' She spoke in firm tones, much as she would to an obstinate child.

Fiona hung up her jacket and went down the hallway to the kitchen, which was located at the back of the cottage.

Greg turned to watch her as she walked past him and disappeared down the hallway. He wondered if she were a mirage, like the wings and pointing finger.

This was Fiona MacDonald? he thought, forcing himself to focus on his present situation. Nah. Couldn't be. The woman he was looking for had to be in her late thirties or so. This woman was barely out of her teens, if that. But then, MacDonald was a fairly common name in Scotland. He rubbed the back of his neck and rolled his head from side to side.

Too bad he'd found the wrong one. It would be too much to hope for that his search would end so easily.

This Fiona MacDonald had vivid red hair that framed her face and tumbled over her shoulders in thick waves. She was no more than a couple of inches over five feet. The top of her head might reach his shoulder…if she stood on her toes.

He shook his head, needing his brain to kick in and start working again. He was exhausted and needed to find a place to sleep. All he'd asked of her were directions. Hadn't he made himself clear?

Greg took a few steps so that he could see into the front room. The comfortably furnished place looked cozy and the warmth lured him closer to the fire. Without further thought, he headed toward the fireplace and held out his chilled hands. Another coughing spell hit him and he quickly covered his mouth.

Once he caught his breath, Greg sank into the wingback chair nearest him. The giant dog watched him from the doorway and Greg wondered if he was being sized up for the monster's next meal.

On the other side of the fireplace a yellow-striped cat stared balefully at him from the arm of an overstuffed chair. A lap robe lay on the other arm and an open book was upside down on the small table nearby.

From the evidence, it looked as though Fiona had been reading while seated in that chair when he arrived. *Great deductive reasoning for a private eye.* His gaze returned to the fire and he squeezed his eyes shut. They burned from fatigue.

A sudden thought made him groan out loud. What if the directions he'd received were for the wrong Fiona MacDonald? Wouldn't that be just the news he needed to round off his day?

He rested his elbow on the arm of the chair and leaned his head against his hand. All his efforts for today had gotten him was thoroughly lost and too tired to care.

The warmth of the room contributed to his drowsiness and he fought to stay awake when all he wanted at the moment was to fall asleep. This would never do. He had to fight whatever was causing his light-headedness. If that woman didn't return soon, he would—

"Here's some tea," Fiona said, interrupting his hazy thoughts. He forced his eyes open. "It should help you to feel better," she added. She held a large ceramic mug toward him, with steam lazily rising.

"I really can't—" he began, but she hushed him with a gesture and gently smiled at him.

Whoa, what was happening here? The way she was standing with the light from the fireplace behind her, she looked as if she glowed. There was no other word to explain it. Her hair shimmered in the light like a halo.

"Drink it," she said softly. "I promise I'm not trying to poison you."

Reluctantly Greg reached for the cup. He brought it to his mouth and sniffed. The stuff didn't smell all that bad, but he'd never been much of a tea drinker. Coffee was his drink of choice. However, it was something hot that might help him to get warm. Besides, she'd been kind enough to make it. The least he could do was to drink it.

The warmth of the mug felt good and he wrapped both hands around it. He hadn't realized how chilled he was until he'd come inside. Greg absently noticed that Fiona sat in the chair across from him. Her cat immediately jumped into her lap while continuing to eye him with disdain.

When the tea had cooled enough, he brought the mug to his lips and sipped, allowing the pleasing warmth of the liquid to slide over his tongue and soothe his throat. He didn't know much about teas, but this one wasn't half-bad. He took another sip and then another. Before long, the mug was empty.

He glanced over at Fiona. "That was quite good, actually," he said politely.

She smiled. "You sound surprised, Mr. Dumas."

Embarrassed, he muttered, "I'm not much of a fan of tea, as a rule." He coughed and hastily set the mug on a nearby table. When he finally managed to control the wracking coughs, he sighed and dropped his head against the back of the chair, closing his eyes once more.

When he opened them sometime later, Fiona stood before him, holding his mug full of fresh tea out to him. "This will help," she said, her voice gentle.

He sighed, looking up at her. She was being very

kind, he thought. The coughing spell had taken so much out of him that he had trouble focusing on her or the mug.

As though she could read his mind, she leaned over and held the warm drink to his lips. He wanted to tell her he wasn't a child, but speech took too much effort at the moment. Greg found it easier to drink the tea in silence.

He rested his eyes as soon as he finished the tea. He knew that she didn't immediately move away from him. The light scent of flowers drifted past him, bringing a vision of sunshine and meadows and happiness and... She must have stepped away because the fragrance gradually dissipated along with the sunshine and happiness.

He needed to thank her for the drink. He needed—

She spoke and her voice sounded far away. He forced himself to open his eyes. She continued to shimmer, as though she were a figment of his imagination. Not even his fertile imagination could have conjured up a woman like this one.

Greg gave his head a shake in an effort to clear his thoughts. It didn't help. Thinking took too much effort. He gave up trying to figure out what she was saying to him. Instead, he allowed himself to drift while he listened to the soothing sound of her lyrical voice.

"It's much too late for you to attempt to find the village tonight, Mr. Dumas. You're not well and you need to rest. Come with me. I have a guest room where you'll be more comfortable.''

She held out her hand and he stared at her for a moment before accepting it. When she tugged, he slowly stood. Greg felt the room shift when he tried to follow her. Something was wrong with him. There was a hum in his head that seemed to drown out all other sounds.

Fiona led him across the room and into the hall. After opening a door across the hallway, she flipped on a switch and quickly moved to the bed.

''Why don't you take off your jacket and shoes?'' she suggested with her angelic smile. He fumbled with the zipper of his leather jacket, but he couldn't make the darned thing work. Must be stuck, he thought. She gently pushed his hands aside and quickly removed his wet jacket. When she motioned to his shoes, he sat on the side of the bed and clumsily removed them.

She walked to the other side of the bed and pulled the covers back. ''I think you'll be comfortable enough here for the night.''

He roused enough to realize what she was saying. ''What did you give me to drink?'' Delayed adrenaline kicked in, somewhat clearing his head. ''You've caused this blurry feeling, haven't you? Who the hell are you?'' he demanded to know before the coughing took over once more.

''We can talk in the morning, Mr. Dumas. You're safe here. Rest,'' she said softly, going to the door. She turned off the light and pulled the door closed, leaving him in darkness.

Greg sat there, wondering how he'd ended up in this woman's bedroom, wondering what she'd given him to make him feel so dopey. His arms felt as if invisible weights held them down. With his last ounce of energy, he removed the rest of his clothing except for his boxer shorts.

He shivered uncontrollably from the chill in the air and curled beneath the covers, their immediate warmth comforting him. All right. The most sensible course would be to stay there for the night, but then he would insist that this woman give him the necessary directions to continue his search for the correct Fiona MacDonald.

That was his last thought before sleep overtook him.

Chapter Two

Fiona woke with a start to the sound of her visitor's breath-stealing cough echoing through the cottage. She glanced at her bedside clock and saw that it was almost five o'clock.

The tea had given him a few hours of rest, which he needed. Not that he would have admitted it. No, sir. Mr. Greg Dumas had certainly been convinced he could continue with his journey.

She sat up, yawning. He needed more of the herbal mixture she had given him. With that in mind, Fiona pulled on her robe and went downstairs to the kitchen, where she mixed the necessary herbs to relieve his cough and congestion, as well as bring down his fever.

While she measured and crushed, her mind wandered into the past.

By the time she was a teenager, she had known that she wanted to help heal people. She had worked with her dad—even though he had retired—with some of the older people who insisted on coming to him for treatment. Because of her interest, he had encouraged her to attend university and to consider medical school, which she had done.

She had left medical school disheartened and more than a little discouraged. She'd learned little to nothing about nutritional needs, preventative medicine or natural remedies that worked as well as pharmaceuticals but with fewer side effects. She and her father had discussed the wide range of healing modalities more than once. Instead of continuing with her medical studies, she'd taken courses in nutrition and natural remedies.

When her parents died, Fiona walked away from her studies and sought a place where she could be alone and come to terms with her loss. She'd stumbled onto Glen Cairn while exploring the Highlands, and on a whim checked to see if there were any available rentals.

The cottage was exactly what she had needed—close enough to people if she wanted to reach out—secluded enough to allow her time to heal. She had never regretted her move.

As word of her training and abilities spread through Glen Cairn, villagers had come to her with their ailments and she had found her grief being eased by helping others.

She'd never told anyone why she was so good at diagnosing illnesses. First, because they wouldn't believe her. Secondly, because she didn't want to be considered odd, as she had been in Craigmor.

The truth was that she saw shimmering colors around each person she met. Over the years she'd learned that certain colors represented physical problems, and certain emotions appeared to her in defining colors, as well. There was no way she could find the words to explain what she saw.

As a child she'd thought that everyone could see those colors and knew what they meant. She'd assumed that was how her father was able to diagnose what was wrong with his patients.

However, as she'd grown older she'd discovered that she was the only one around who witnessed what she saw. After being laughed at several times, she'd learned to keep quiet about seeing colors that no one else appeared to detect.

Instead, she used her knowledge and skills to diagnose and treat others with her home-grown herbs, salves and her intuitive messages.

Fiona poured the steeped herbal tea, let it cool

a bit and took it to her guest bedroom. After tapping on the door and getting no response, she quietly turned the knob and walked into the bedroom. Rather than turn on the overhead light, she reached for a small lamp near the door. Once there was light, she turned and looked at her guest.

The covers were bunched around his waist, displaying his bare chest. He lay on his back, his head turned away from her, his latest coughing spell still echoing in the room.

"I've brought you some tea."

He slowly turned his head toward her and the light, his eyes appearing unfocused.

She touched his arm and discovered that he was burning up. She gave his shoulder a light shake. "Can you sit up for me, please?"

He blinked. When his eyes opened a second time, they were somewhat clearer. "What do you want?" he asked, his words slurred.

"I want you to drink this," she replied, sitting on the edge of the bed and offering him the cup.

He came up on one elbow and took the cup, draining it as though he was thirsty. Without a word he handed it back to her and fell back on the bed.

She smiled, almost amused at his change in attitude. Perhaps he was too sick to care what she gave him. Fiona went over to the tall dresser in the corner and opened one of the drawers. She pulled out a large flannel shirt and brought it back to the bed.

"Here. Put this on…. You need to stay warm."

Greg opened his eyes and frowned at her. "I'm hot. I don't need a shirt."

"Take my word for it. You really do need to keep your chest warm."

His frown grew, but he sat up and pulled the shirt over his head without another word. With a glare that spoke volumes, he rolled over so that his back was to her and said, "Turn out the light when you leave."

He sounded as gruff as a grizzly disturbed in his rest. She may not know much about her visitor, but he'd made it clear he would not be an easy patient to look after.

She turned on a night-light, turned off the lamp and returned to the kitchen to find the salve she needed for his chest.

McTavish had followed her downstairs and now sat just inside the kitchen door, giving her a disgruntled look. "Yes, I know," she said soothingly. "I have disturbed your rest, as well. Go back upstairs. I'll be there shortly."

With a muffled snort the dog went into the hallway, pausing for a moment in front of the stairs to glance at the closed bedroom door before he trotted up them. Sometimes he acted as if he understood every word she said.

Perhaps he did, she thought.

Fiona quietly reentered the guest bedroom with the jar and more tea. The night-light cast enough of a glow for her to see the bed and nearby table. She placed the items on the table and sat beside him on the bed.

Once again he lay sprawled on his back, his arms thrown wide. When she brushed her hand against his forehead, she knew she had to do whatever was necessary to break his fever.

His immune system was struggling and needed help. No doubt Mr. Dumas pushed himself beyond his physical limits on a regular basis, which made him human, she supposed, but didn't help when an infection managed to overcome him. He had little energy in reserve to combat his illness.

She reached for the ointment.

He stirred, turning his face toward her. "Jill?" he murmured. "I've missed you so much." He took Fiona's hand and tugged her toward him. She managed to catch her balance enough not to fall directly on him. Instead, she now lay next to him, her head on his shoulder.

"Mr. Dumas," she said softly. "We need to bring your fever down. I'm also going to rub an ointment on your chest to ease the congestion there."

She pulled away from him and reached for the cup.

He didn't let go of her hand. "Jill?" He sounded puzzled.

"No. My name is Fiona."

She pulled her hand away from him and slid her arm beneath his head, raising him slightly. He opened his eyes without a sign of recognition before closing them again.

Fiona held the cup to his lips. "This will help your cough and your fever, I promise."

He drank as greedily as he had earlier. Once he finished, she returned the empty cup to the table and lowered his head back to the pillow.

She picked up the jar again and took out a dollop of the salve with her fingers. She cupped the ointment in her hands to warm the soft mixture. When the creamy medication reached body temperature she lifted his shirt and stroked her hand across his chest.

A charge of energy shot through her hand and arm, catching her off guard. She felt as if she'd just stuck her finger into a live electrical socket.

Greg Dumas was a powerful man regardless of his present condition. At least he was having a powerful effect on *her*. She forced herself to move her hand with a calmness she was far from feeling and applied the soothing mixture over his chest.

He smiled without opening his eyes. The smile unnerved her. She smoothed the ointment more swiftly, wanting to be finished with this part of the healing process. His chest was broad and muscled, and touching him created a fluttery feeling inside her, a sensation she was unused to experiencing.

Fiona made certain she'd covered the area adequately before she withdrew her hand from beneath his shirt. Or tried to. As soon as she began to withdraw, he trapped her hand beneath his.

As calmly as she could, Fiona said, "You need to rest now, Mr. Dumas. It's early yet. Try to sleep a few more hours."

He opened his eyes. They glittered in the faint light. He stared at her for a moment before he said, "I'll sleep but I want you here beside me."

He no longer sounded like a bear. Instead, he had become a virile male who knew what he wanted, and at the moment he wanted her in his bed.

Fiona had never run into this situation before. For one thing, she'd never had an occasion to treat a male without another family member being present. For another, she had never expected any male, regardless of his fevered condition, to show a personal interest in her.

"I don't believe that would be a good idea," she finally replied, speaking as softly and soothingly as possible. The man had no idea what he was saying and probably wouldn't remember any of this once he recovered from his illness.

In the meantime…she wasn't sure what to do.

Greg took matters into his own hands, literally, by pulling her toward him until she tumbled onto the bed beside him. With a grin that enhanced his attractiveness, he wrapped his arms around her.

"Now I'll sleep," he said, as though keeping a promise.

The man was much stronger than she'd realized. Fiona wasn't certain she could get up without a struggle. Her most startling realization was that she was in no way frightened of him, despite the fact that she'd never been this close to a male other than her father.

She forced herself to relax, hoping he would release his hold on her. The tea she'd given him should ease him into sleep in a few minutes.

He turned his face toward hers and nuzzled her neck.

"Mmm," he murmured, "you smell nice."

She froze in disbelief. He flicked his tongue along her earlobe, causing her to shiver. When he slipped his hand beneath her robe and gown and stroked her bare breast, she almost strangled on her gasp. He made a sound of contentment as he continued to stroke and caress her, causing her nipple to pucker in the palm of his hand. A surge of pure sensual pleasure swept over her.

Fiona panicked. She could not allow this to continue. He would be horribly embarrassed later on— as would she!—when he recalled what he had done.

Greg nibbled on her ear before he licked it again.

"Mr. Dumas," she managed to say when she was able to catch her breath. "You really need to rest."

He ignored her and trailed kisses along her neck and the curve of her shoulder. "Stay with me," he whispered, his husky voice vibrating in her ear. "I've missed you so much, sweetheart. There were times when I thought I'd die from the pain of losing you. But you're here now. Stay with me and let me love you."

Finally, the soporific effect of the tea kicked in and his hand slid away from her breast. She swallowed, willing her heart and breathing to slow down.

Fiona carefully left the bed, watching him with a combination of dismay and an unexpected yearning she'd never experienced before. His thick dark hair fell across his forehead. His face was flushed with fever and Fiona had an almost uncontrollable urge to push his hair away from his face and thread her fingers through its silky softness.

She knew better than to act on her impulse. She slipped out of the bedroom before temptation became too much for her to resist and hurried to the kitchen. She needed a dose of her own herbal tea to soothe and relax her.

While she sipped from her cup a few minutes later, Fiona reminded herself that Greg hadn't known what he was doing. His fever had climbed rapidly since he'd gone to bed, which wasn't a good sign.

She was worried about him. She gathered up supplies, including tea and ointments, and returned to his room. She felt she needed to keep a closer eye on his condition.

Fiona found him restlessly moving his legs, muttering incomprehensibly. He said the name Jill several times, as though she were there. He was talking to her, pleading with her.

His fever needed to come down. Fiona had mixed stronger herbs to help contain the infection that was causing the fever.

She sat beside him and said, "Mr. Dumas... please drink this." She slipped her arm beneath his head, held the cup to his lips and managed to get him to drink without spilling it.

Once the cup was drained, she stepped away from him. She knew she wouldn't be able to sleep, knowing that the infection appeared to have progressed enough to overcome him.

Fiona settled into a large overstuffed chair in the corner of the room. Within minutes McTavish showed up at the door. He watched her for a moment before he ambled across the room to the chair where she was. He stretched out on the floor in front of her, forming a footrest for her.

She pulled a blanket around her shoulders and began her wait for her newest patient to respond to the medications.

* * *

He couldn't breathe.

A heavy weight rested on his chest, forcing him to push hard to get air into his lungs.

He coughed and a sharp pain shot through his chest.

Something was wrong with him.

The painful coughing continued, stealing what little breath he managed to get.

A voice murmured nearby. Soft hands cooled his body with a moist cloth that caused him to shiver.

"Jill?" he whispered hoarsely.

"It's Fiona. Drink this…it will help."

A soothing liquid trickled into his mouth and down his parched throat. He relaxed and allowed the moisture to ease his dry throat.

Fiona. He'd heard that name before. Did he know a Fiona? He couldn't recall.

Oh. He remembered now. He was looking for a Fiona. He couldn't remember why, but he knew finding her was important.

He must have found her. That was good because he had to get home.

Tina needed him.

Jill needed him.

No. It was too late to help Jill. He couldn't do anything to save her.

Jill was dead. It was his fault.

Now he paid the price for not saving her. He'd been doomed to the fiery flames of hell for all eternity. He could feel the flames singeing him, sucking the air from his lungs.

He'd sometimes wondered if hell was a real place. Now he could tell the world it existed. It hurt. The heat was consuming him.

A young girl kept visiting him—offering him drinks, checking his temperature, bathing him, helping him with his personal needs.

He should be embarrassed. He didn't know this girl but somehow it didn't matter. What had she done to be consigned to hell? Must have been bad to have to experience this. Poor thing.

He was tired, much too tired to ask her why she was there.

Images of a strange bedroom flitted periodically through his world. At times the room would be so bright the light hurt his eyes, sunlight from a nearby window filling the area. Other times—only a minute or so later, wasn't it?—the room had no light, just shadows moving around him. The light and lack of light did nothing to stop the flames that kept licking at him.

Greg saw the gun. He signaled to Jill to get out of the store before the stupid punk with the .38 spotted her.

Where had the other gunman come from? The patrol car should be here by now.

A spray of bullets shattered the glass around him. He had to stop the shooter. He had to check on Jill.

Blood. So much blood.

"Dear God," he whispered brokenly. "Jill."

"You're dreaming. You're safe here. You're going to be all right. Just rest."

The voice came to him—peaceful and soothing. "Tina?"

"Fiona. I won't leave you. Allow the medications to work on you. You're doing fine. You're safe," she repeated.

Of course he was safe. It was Jill he'd left unguarded.

Fiona knew that tonight would be the crisis. Three nights had passed since her visitor had arrived. She had stayed with him 'round the clock except for short breaks to eat and bathe. When he was quiet, she managed to nap in the chair in his room. There were times when he would have lucid moments before falling back all too often into some nightmarish scene that haunted him.

She lost track of time. She measured her hours by bathing him with cool water to bring his fever down. Was his cough sounding less congested? Were his lungs taking in more air? She wasn't certain. All she knew was that she couldn't leave him to fight his battle alone.

His fever broke somewhere between four and five o'clock the morning of the fourth day, and Greg slipped into a deep, healing sleep.

Fiona was exhausted.

She forced herself to climb the stairs to her room, pulling herself up each step by hanging on to the handrail. With the last of her reserves, Fiona stumbled into her room, found her nightgown and dropped into bed.

She immediately slept.

Chapter Three

A steady rapping caused Fiona to stir. As she finally surfaced from exhausted sleep, she realized she had been hearing the noise for some time. Disoriented, she opened her eyes and looked around. Sunlight poured through the windows. She blinked. She didn't usually sleep past sunup.

Then she remembered Greg and the past few days and nights. She hadn't heard him cough in the past few hours. She hoped it was because he'd been resting better and not because she'd been too tired to hear him.

Fiona looked at the clock and groaned. It was

after three o'clock in the afternoon and someone was at the door.

McTavish hadn't barked, which meant it was someone they knew.

She went to the bedroom window and peered out just as she heard a feminine voice saying, "Fiona, dear, please answer the door. I really must speak with you."

Mrs. Cavendish.

Oh, dear. Sarah Cavendish was an absolute dear without a hint of malice in her soul. Unfortunately she was also the biggest gossip in the entire glen. Fiona had no compunction about explaining to anyone how she had spent the past few days and nights, but she would prefer to do so once she had caught up on her sleep and her thinking processes were more clear.

Well, it couldn't be helped. Mrs. Cavendish was here now. The rental car gave mute evidence of the presence of a visitor. Before dark the entire village would know that Fiona had company. There was no need for newspapers and television with Mrs. Cavendish around.

"Just a moment, Mrs. Cavendish," she called from her window. "I'll be right with you." She turned away and spotted McTavish, who watched her from where he lay sprawled on the braided rug beside her bed.

"Fine watchdog you are," she scolded, grabbing the first clothes she could find. "You could have given me some warning, you know.'' Dressed in a sweater and trousers but still in her slippers, Fiona hurried downstairs to let Mrs. Cavendish in.

She paused to take a couple of deep breaths before she opened the door with what she hoped was a serene smile.

Mrs. Cavendish stood there looking bewildered by the delay, holding a large, obviously heavy basket. ''Oh, Mrs. Cavendish,'' Fiona said contritely, feeling convicted for leaving the poor woman standing at the door for so long. ''I didn't hear you right away.'' She stepped back so that Sarah could come inside. ''Let me take your basket.''

''Oh, thank you,'' Sarah replied with heartfelt relief. ''I was so afraid I would drop it. I had the mister drop me off at the beginning of your lane, thinking I wouldn't mind a good walk. I swear the basket took on an ounce or more with each step.''

Because her hands were full, Fiona bumped her hip against the door until it closed. ''You must be chilled,'' she said. ''Let's go into the kitchen and I'll make us some tea.''

Once in the kitchen, Sarah sat at the small table before asking, ''Did I catch you at a bad time, dear?''

Fiona continued to measure out tea while waiting for the kettle to boil. She didn't look around. ''Why, no. This is fine.''

''Oh.'' There was silence. ''Well. I just wondered. Your hair is a little tumbled and you have your sweater on wrong side out.''

Fiona closed her eyes, wondering if she should explain why she looked as if she'd just gotten up. Was it really anyone's business?

She wouldn't be feeling so guilty if she hadn't shared such an intimate moment with Greg the night he arrived. She needed to place what happened into perspective. He was ill and had been out of his head with fever. The matter was simple when looked at from that perspective. Unfortunately her emotions weren't rational at the moment.

She forced a laugh that sounded exactly that—forced. She turned and ran her fingers through her hair, wincing at a tangle.

''I hadn't realized,'' she finally muttered. ''How silly of me. If you'll excuse me, I'll set myself to rights while the tea steeps.''

Not waiting for a response, Fiona hurried out of the kitchen and up the stairs once again. She closed her bedroom door and sighed. From there she could see her reflection in her dresser mirror. Her hair looked as though it had been styled by an electric mixer.

She hauled her sweater over her head, grabbed a bra from her lingerie drawer and put it on, and then she carefully turned the sweater right side out before slipping it back over her shoulders. She hurried into the bathroom, brushed her hair, pulled it back with a couple of combs, splashed water on her face, dried it and returned downstairs.

Sarah was pouring their tea. She had set out a pound cake and sliced off a couple of pieces. After setting the cups and saucers on the table, she put the slices on Fiona's dessert plates and beamed at her.

"I baked a couple of these this morning and thought you might like to have one of them," she said, motioning Fiona to sit. "Plus I brought you some fresh eggs and some homemade loaves of bread. I always make too much and I figured you don't have much time for baking with all that you do."

Fiona picked up her cup and drank, needing something in her stomach. She couldn't remember when she last ate. Cake wouldn't have been her first choice for nourishment, but it was better than nothing. She suddenly realized that she was starved.

"Thank you for finishing making the tea. I appreciate your bringing me the eggs and baked goods. It was very kind of you."

Sarah flushed with pleasure. "Well, you do so much for all of us, dear, that I felt it was only fair to give something back."

Fiona smiled. "I'm amply paid for my services, Mrs. Cavendish."

Sarah waved that comment away. "Nonsense. You don't charge nearly enough for the hours you put in. Why, Terese mentioned just the other day how you stayed with her two boys until whatever they had released its grip on them. I don't know how you do it. You perform miracles every day.''

''Not at all. Remember my father was a physician and I've had training in the medical field.''

Sarah raised her brows. ''He didn't teach you about all those things you grow in the garden that you turn into tea and ointments, now, did he?''

''No, he didn't,'' Fiona admitted with a smile. ''I attended additional classes to learn the medicinal qualities of the herbs I use. I find natural remedies to be a great help in healing.'' She rose and brought the teapot to the table. She filled both cups once more before she reseated herself and tasted the pound cake. It absolutely melted in her mouth. Why not, she thought, with all the sugar and butter used in it. She could feel her arteries clogging with each bite.

The two chatted for several minutes before Sarah glanced at her watch. ''Oh, my, I hadn't realized the time. I need to start back while there's still some light.''

They both stood. ''Thank you again for all the goodies,'' Fiona said. ''I can already see the weight I'll gain, but I must admit it will be worth it.''

Sarah laughed. ''Nonsense. You're a skinny little thing and you know it. It would do you no harm to put on a few pounds.'' With an arch look, she added, "The laddies do enjoy a curvaceous lass, you know."

Not that again. Every woman in the village was determined to play matchmaker for her, whether she wanted one or not.

She walked Mrs. Cavendish to the front door. When Fiona opened it, Sarah took a step forward and paused. "I'm getting more and more forgetful in my old age, I declare. I meant to ask you when I first arrived. Whose car is that? As soon as you opened the door, I completely forgot."

"Well," she began, "I...uh—"

She was interrupted by the sound of coughing coming from the guest bedroom. Despite being flustered by the need to explain Greg's presence, she was relieved to hear his cough sounding much better.

Sarah's eyes rounded. "My goodness. Someone sounds really sick in there. I didn't realize you had a patient or I wouldn't have kept you so long."

Fiona smiled. "Yes, as a matter of fact I do need to prepare more tea for that cough."

Sarah nodded. "Well, I won't keep you. Is your patient from the village? I don't recognize the car."

"Um, no. No, he's not. He's from—"

"He? You have a *man* in your house? Oh, my, Fiona, do you think that's wise? You should have called one of us and we could have come to stay here with you."

"That wasn't necessary, Mrs. Cavendish. He has been much too sick to be a threat to anyone." It was unfortunate that she should recall at that particular moment his hand caressing her breast. She knew her face turned red at the memory.

Mrs. Cavendish never missed a thing. She nodded her head with a knowing smile. "Oooh, it's that way, is it? Well, I won't keep you." She turned away and strode rapidly toward the lane.

Fiona closed the door. McTavish stood in front of the stairwell with a plaintive expression. "Yes, I know you're starving to death as we speak. Let me check on our patient first, then I'll feed you while I'm making more tea for him."

She peeked into the bedroom and saw that Greg was still asleep. She walked to the bed and studied him. His color was much better than it had been, his fever had come down and his breathing no longer sounded labored.

Greg was officially on the mend. It was time for a light meal to help him regain his strength.

McTavish followed her into the kitchen. She fed him and let him outside before quickly preparing some porridge and dry toast. Before she finished, McTavish scratched at the door to return inside. "Oh, so you're back on guard duty, are you?" she asked in a low voice.

McTavish gave her a doggy smile and lifted his paw.

She shook her head ruefully. She wasn't certain

who was in charge of whom in this household. She glanced up in time to see Tiger sashay through the doorway. No doubt the timing of his entrance was staged as a reminder that *he* was king of this particular castle.

He sniffed his bowl and looked around, his expression speaking volumes. "All right! But you're a long way from starving, mister."

After feeding Tiger, she placed Greg's meal on a tray and went down the hallway. Fiona balanced the tray with one hand and tapped on the door with the other.

There was no answer. She opened the door and said, "Mr. Dumas?"

This time he stirred enough to reply.

"Come in," Greg said hoarsely. The effort started him coughing. Yes, the cough sounded much better, but was no doubt still painful.

She opened the door and found him lying propped up in bed, a look of bewilderment on his face.

"Good afternoon," she said, smiling. She placed the tray on the bedside table. "I've brought you something easy to digest to start you eating again. I hope you're hungry."

He stared at her, frowning. "What's going on? I don't understand what I'm doing here, or where here is…and who are you?"

"You're in Glen Cairn, Mr. Dumas. You've been quite ill these past few days. I brought you a little something to eat as well as more tea for your cough and remaining congestion.'' She picked up the tea and held it out to him.

He looked at the cup as though it might contain hemlock. He must be feeling better. He was responding as he had that first night, back to his suspicious self. She felt giddy with relief.

Greg glanced at her, then back to the cup in her hands. ''How did I get here?'' he asked, without taking the tea she offered.

''I believe you got lost and turned up my lane for directions.'' She leaned closer, holding the tea out toward him. ''This will help your cough continue to improve, if you'd care to take it.''

He clutched the covers to his chest with one hand and slowly took the drink with the other. He sniffed. Since she had added cinnamon to give the drink a more pleasing scent and taste, he not only looked relieved but pleasantly surprised by the familiar odor. He took a tentative sip.

She knew the liquid would feel good to his dry mouth and raw throat. He continued to drink until the mug was empty.

Fiona handed him the porridge, which he took with more interest. It didn't take him long to empty the bowl.

He looked around the room. ''I, uh, I need to use your bathroom.''

She nodded. ''There's a small one beneath the

stairs just outside the room. Do you need help getting there?''

He glared at her. "No. What I need is some privacy. All I'm wearing is somebody's shirt and my underpants.''

His modesty caught her off guard. He must have no memory of her bathing him. On the other hand, it was reassuring to know that he would probably never remember caressing her and trying to coax her into bed with him. Hopefully, if he remembered anything, he would place it with the fevered dreams he'd been having.

She nodded, hoping he didn't see that his comment had flustered her. From the way he said it, he must think that she had undressed him.

Without a word, she walked out of the room and back to the kitchen. She needed something to eat besides pound cake, and from the grouchy attitude of her guest, he might be ready for more porridge, as well.

She heard a bump and a couple of swear words, then silence. Eventually she heard the bedroom door open. She refused to check on him. If he fell flat on his face, she'd deal with him then.

Instead she placed two bowls of porridge on the table and made toast.

She'd just finished the toast when she heard a slight sound and looked around to see Greg leaning against the doorjamb of the kitchen. He looked around the room as though he'd never seen anything like it.

She'd forgotten how tall he was. Now that the fever had left him, he was pale. His hair was rumpled and he had a good start on a beard.

Fiona fought not to smile at him. She found him adorable, all growly and defensive. She had a strong hunch that Greg hated feeling weak and shaky. Naturally, he'd attempt to cover his present condition by sounding tough.

She found his belligerence understandable, but she didn't have to placate him, regardless of his mood. She did not want to think about how strongly this man's presence affected her.

Heated color warmed her cheeks at the thought and she turned away. "I've made you another bowl of porridge," she said, placing the plate of toast on the table. "Then I suggest you return to bed. You're going to need some time to recover your strength."

"Look, are you keeping me captive here or something?"

She stepped back from the table and stared at him. "What?"

"I don't understand what's going on here." He hadn't moved from the doorway.

She looked from him to the table. "I'm offering to feed you. I fail to see anything sinister in that." She sat and began to butter her toast.

He moved silently across the room until he stood

across from her, only the table separating them. "You aren't answering my questions."

She took a bite of toast, chewed and swallowed before she replied, "Some of your questions are too ridiculous to address."

He pulled out a chair and sat down. "Wanting to know your name is ridiculous?"

"Oh. Well, no, not that one. My name is Fiona MacDonald." She offered him the butter.

He absently took it, frowning. "I'm looking for a woman by that name," he finally said.

"So you mentioned when you first arrived."

He rubbed his brow. "I don't remember much about that. I seem to recall bits and pieces of things, but that's all."

"You've been here four days, Mr. Dumas."

"Four days! How could that be?"

"You've been battling an infection that settled in your chest. Hopefully the teas I prepared for you and the ointment I used on your chest have been able to help you fight the infection."

"Are you a doctor or something?"

She nodded. "Or something, yes. I've been doing what I can to help you. Something has obviously worked because you're sitting here eating. However, you'll find that although you're feeling better, you're going to be weak for a few days. You'll need to rest and recuperate or you'll take the chance of having a relapse."

He finished his second bowl of porridge, toast

and tea before he said, "I don't have time to rest. I need to get to the village and find the woman I'm looking for."

"I thought I was the one you were looking for."

He stared at her for a moment, his eyes narrowed. After a moment he shook his head. "No, I don't think so. Is Fiona a common name in Scotland?"

"Not so common, particularly coupled with MacDonald."

He rubbed his forehead again. "Well, you can't be the woman I'm looking for. She's probably in her mid- to late-thirties, possibly older."

"Is your head bothering you?"

"What? Oh. Yeah, I guess it is."

"I would imagine your fever is coming up again, as well. Why don't you go lie down now?"

"Haven't you heard a word I've said? I don't have time to lie around in bed. I need to go to Glen Cairn and find this woman!"

Fiona clasped her hands before her and said, "Mr. Dumas. I am the only Fiona MacDonald living in or around Glen Cairn. And you, sir, are swaying in your chair to such an extent that I fear you're going to pass out at any moment. I would greatly appreciate it if you would be so kind as to allow me to escort you back to bed. It would be a great deal easier for me than dragging you, unconscious, through my home!"

Chapter Four

Greg stared in astonishment at the wisp of a woman seated across from him. He felt as though a harmless, cuddly kitten had attacked him with bared teeth and claws.

His head continued to pound so ferociously that he could scarcely hear her. The only thing he wanted to do at the moment was to lie down—which was exactly what this Fiona had suggested. So why was he sitting there in a vain attempt to be macho?

He carefully stood without answering her and walked with all the dignity he could muster to the kitchen door. Once around the corner and into the hallway he slumped against the wall, praying he made it to the bedroom without disgracing himself by collapsing in the hall. He had a vision of Fiona daintily stepping over his inert body without a glance on her way to another part of the house.

Her behemoth dog appeared around the corner from the front room and eyed him thoughtfully. Greg watched with growing dismay as the dog ambled toward him. When it reached him, the dog turned around and leaned slightly into Greg. He realized with a start that the dog was offering to help him.

Greg placed his hand gingerly at first then more firmly against the dog's back. It took his weight without strain. Step by step the two of them went down the hallway. Greg had one arm braced on the wall and the other on the dog.

The dog paused at the bedroom doorway, allowing Greg to walk through before he entered behind him.

"Thanks, pal," Greg muttered. He made it to the bed and slumped on the edge. At the moment, he felt as if he'd have to get better to die. A bed had never held more appeal for him. He grimaced. Except on his honeymoon, he supposed, but he had no intention of dredging up *those* memories.

He tugged his clothes off and wearily slid beneath the covers. When he turned onto his side he spotted a pitcher and a glass of water. He leaned on his elbow and picked up the glass. The water helped to relieve the dryness of his mouth and soothed his raw throat.

When he replaced his glass on the table, he noticed that the dog had not left the bedroom. It sat watching him with a steady gaze.

"What's your name, pal?"

The dog continued to eye him, Greg swore, with amusement at the idea that a human would expect a dog to answer him.

"McTavish."

Greg had been in the process of rolling onto his back when he heard the name. He jerked his head around and saw Fiona standing inside the door holding a tray. Okay, so his mind was playing tricks on him. Besides, a dog that size wouldn't have such a feminine voice.

"Hello, McTavish," he said, nodding politely to the dog, feeling as though he'd found an ally in this household.

Fiona set the tray next to the bed. It held a steaming cup. She refilled the water glass and handed him two capsules.

He took them from the palm of her hand and stared at them.

"If my intentions were to poison you, Mr. Dumas, I could have done so at any time during the past four days."

He glanced at her for a moment in silence. "Are you always so waspish?" he finally asked.

"Only with cantankerous patients. At the moment you are at the top of that list."

He nodded. "Just wondered." He looked back at the capsules. "Would it be cantankerous of me to ask what these are for?"

"I would like to say they aid in improving your disposition, but I haven't come up with a formula for that one yet. Those are pain relievers that can be bought at any store. They're for your headache."

"And the tea?" he asked, with what he hoped was the necessary politeness she expected from him.

"The tea is what has assisted you in overcoming the infection you've been battling. I have also mixed up the necessary herbs to help your cough in case you need it. If you start coughing again, drink some of this tea.

"The best thing you can do for yourself at the moment is to take the capsules, drink the tea and continue to rest," she said briskly. "You'll feel better in the next day or so, I should think."

"Yes, ma'am," he replied meekly, his eyes lowered.

She abruptly broke into peals of delighted laughter, the sound echoing in the room like a melodic shower of notes. Her laughter was contagious and he found himself chuckling hoarsely in response, which triggered another coughing episode.

She left the room without a word.

He expected McTavish to follow but the dog remained where he was. Greg picked up the mug and sipped it to check the temperature, which was not too hot, before he drank it in its entirety. His tickling throat, which triggered his need to cough, subsided with the soothing liquid but the previous coughing spell and his efforts to suppress it had used up the small amount of energy he had.

Fiona reappeared, carrying a teapot. "I apologize for laughing, but your fake humility was too much for me." She poured more tea. "Drink as much as you can. It will help your cough."

He nodded. "What makes you think it was fake?" he asked, his voice raspy. It hurt to talk. Hell, it hurt to breathe, but he didn't care for the only other option he had.

She tilted her head slightly and Greg realized with a start that Fiona was a very attractive woman. His idea of beauty had always been a tall woman with dark hair and eyes. He'd admired Jill's tall, curvaceous body and Tina already showed signs of being tall for her age.

Fiona was small, probably weighing no more than a hundred pounds or so. She wasn't much over five feet tall. Her hair was thick and wavy. In some lights it looked fiery red. Other times it was more golden.

She had eyes the color of the sea, and just as changeable. At times they appeared gray. At other times, they looked deep blue-green. Glowing with laughter they'd become a light blue, almost silvery. Her eyes gave away her emotions.

He wondered what color they were when she made love? He indulged in a brief fantasy until he saw her flush, as though she could read his thoughts.

His fever must be back, otherwise why would he have such a preposterous thought?

"I can't imagine that you have ever been filled with humility."

A dark memory pushed its way into his thoughts and he shook his head to dislodge it. "Don't count on it," he muttered, and sipped the tea.

"I'm sorry. I didn't mean to be so personal," she said quietly.

She turned and went to the door, pausing long enough to say, "Come, McTavish. Allow Mr. Dumas to rest."

Without moving, McTavish gave Greg a soulful look with his large brown eyes.

"I don't mind if he stays," Greg said between sips of tea.

She threw up her hands and left, muttering something that sounded like "Men!" As soon as the door closed behind her, McTavish pushed himself to his feet, meandered to the side of the bed and, with a lightness Greg found astonishing, sprang up on the bed and lowered himself next to Greg.

Greg worked hard to control what would have

been a shout of laughter at McTavish's smug expression. No use giving away the actions of his newfound friend. Greg stroked the massive head and was rewarded with a contented sigh.

He took another sip of the tea and yawned. He didn't know what was in the drink, but it acted like a knockout drug. Or maybe it had such a strong effect on him because he'd been knocked off his feet with this illness.

His mother-in-law rarely let a day pass when he came to pick up Tina that she didn't mention how much he needed to take some time off…how he needed to rest more often…how he needed to take better care of himself.

He was glad she had no way of knowing that he was paying the price for ignoring her advice. When he got around to telling her, he knew he'd never hear the end of it.

Greg closed his eyes and allowed himself to drift into sleep, comforted by the sound of McTavish's heavy breathing beside him.

A couple of hours later Fiona peeked into her patient's room. He and McTavish had become buddies rather quickly, it seemed. They both slept soundly, Greg's arm thrown over McTavish's back.

She could count on McTavish to keep his eye on her charge while she made a quick trip to the village.

Once outside, she decided to get Greg's clothes out of his car. Thank goodness he hadn't bothered to lock it when he'd arrived. She found a suitcase and a briefcase and took them inside.

Fiona opened the bedroom door and stepped inside, placing the suitcase on the floor near the dresser and the briefcase on a table. McTavish raised his head and looked at her, as though daring her to suggest he leave their patient.

Fiona gave him a small wave and retreated to the door. Satisfied, McTavish sighed and put his head down once again.

The weather had cleared but the wind was brisk. Although she generally walked, Fiona chose to drive today so that she would be back sooner. She had errands to run and provisions to buy since she would be feeding another. In addition, she wanted to hear how the village had responded to Sarah Cavendish's most recent newsflash.

She did not look forward to being the latest subject of speculation. On the other hand, with a man unknown to the villagers staying in her home, she might be taken off the matchmakers' lists.

Her visit lasted longer than she'd expected and it was dark when Fiona returned home. Since there were no lights on in the house, she suspected Greg was still asleep.

Rest was the best thing for him. The body naturally healed itself if given a chance. She would guess that Mr. Dumas had been overtaxing his body for some time. Sooner or later, the body rebels against continued abuse. That looked to be what had happened to him.

McTavish greeted her when she opened the back door.

"Ah, so you finished your nap, did you?" she asked, nudging the door closed behind her. She set the groceries on the kitchen table. Tiger jumped down from the windowsill and practiced his snake dance around and between her ankles, making it more difficult for her to put the items away without tripping.

"Yes, yes, I know. You are on the verge of starvation, as well. It's terrible how both you and McTavish are so mistreated. Yes, yes, I understand. You won't last another hour if you aren't fed immediately."

Fiona finally managed to put the food away and immediately fed her companions.

As usual, Tiger ate with fastidious precision while McTavish refused to slow down to savor his meal. Instead, he seemed to inhale it, his large tongue making short work of cleaning his bowl. In his case, quantity most definitely outweighed quality.

Fiona made a thick broth and some bread rolls, wondering if her guest would like them. She grinned, thinking about his feigned meekness earlier today. She also recalled his smile of pure deviltry.

She needed to face the fact that Greg Dumas's presence in her home could be lethal to her peace of mind. She had seen the strong emotions that he controlled but she knew nothing about his life or what triggered those emotions. She didn't know, for instance, if he was married or not. All she knew was that his calling her Jill told her there was a lover in his life who was important to him.

She had no reason to be disheartened by the idea. He was a very attractive man, after all. It would be much more unusual if he weren't married.

Besides, he would be leaving once he regained his health. She paused. Come to think of it, she'd never asked him why he was looking for her. Fiona could think of no reason why an American would want to contact her. She had never visited the United States, nor did she know anyone who lived there.

Until now.

Fiona sighed, feeling like an infatuated schoolgirl mooning over her literature teacher. It was time to face facts. Greg had made it abundantly clear that she was nothing more than an irritant in his life.

Once the meal was prepared, Fiona placed everything on a tray and took it to her visitor. The door stood ajar, no doubt thanks to McTavish's earlier exit. Since the tray she held was large and filled to capacity, Fiona eased the opening wider with her shoulder without knocking and walked into the room...in time to see Greg clad only in his underwear in the process of pulling on a pair of denim jeans.

"Oh! I'm so sorry. I should have knocked," she said, turning away from him and setting the tray on the dresser. With her back turned, she said, "You really need to stay in bed."

She heard his disgusted sigh. "I'm aware that you believe that. However, I'm not used to lying around like this. I don't remember ever sleeping so much in my life. Whatever you've been giving me has been knocking me out for hours at a time and I don't like it." Belligerence echoed in his tone.

He appeared beside her and she was relieved to see that he now wore a thick sweater and a pair of boots in addition to his jeans. He had found his suitcase.

"If you intend to stay up, I'll take your supper back to the kitchen," she said, ignoring his remark.

He turned away and walked to the door. "Suit yourself. I need to shave." He moved out of her sight and she heard his quiet footfalls as he walked down the hall.

Once she heard the bathroom door close, she sagged into a nearby chair and fanned her heated cheeks. Oh my, bathing him when he was semi-conscious was one thing. Seeing him fully awake with next to nothing on was quite different.

He had a beautiful body; there was no other way to describe it. From his wide shoulders and narrow waist to his hips and muscled thighs, Mr. Dumas could have been the model for a Greek statue.

In the lamplight, his bare chest had gleamed— the taut muscles rippling from his chest to the top of his low-slung shorts. Fiona shivered at the memory. She could no longer deny to herself that she was attracted to this stranger. However, she had no intention of acting on that attraction. The last thing she wanted was for him to know how easily her emotions were stirred by him.

When Greg walked into the kitchen, Fiona had already set the table and placed his broth there. She poured them some water and motioned for him to be seated.

''Where's McTavish?'' he asked, looking around, as though nervous without his newfound companion.

''He's out patrolling the perimeter,'' she replied with a smile. ''He considers that to be one of his duties in guarding me. Of course he also gets the opportunity to exercise. He needs to run every day to rid himself of pent-up energy.''

''Wish I had that problem,'' Greg muttered. He looked at Fiona. ''He didn't get much of that today. When I woke up, he was still with me.''

She nodded. ''He was guarding you while I was away.''

''You left?'' he asked, his eyes narrowing.

"I needed some supplies." She nodded toward his broth. "You need to have a few things I'd run out of."

He stared at the bowl in front of him, then glanced up. "I'll reimburse you for what you've had to spend on me." His voice sounded flat.

She met his gaze before quietly saying, "I was explaining why I was gone, not hinting that I feel you owe me for anything."

He shook his head. "Doesn't matter. I pay my own way. You've obviously taken care of me while I was sick, as well as provided me with a place to sleep. Now you're feeding me."

She leaned back in her chair. "You know, if you really want to help me, why don't you tell me why you're looking for me."

"I've already explained—" he began.

She stopped him. "All right. Tell me about the woman you're looking for."

"I'm looking for the daughter of Dr.—"

"—James MacDonald of Craigmor, isn't that so?"

His startled expression answered her.

"I am his daughter and, as you can see, I'm not in my mid- to late-thirties. Why did you suppose I was?"

He continued to stare at her. "I was told that he was in his seventies when he died. I figured that his daughter would have to be—" He paused and waved his hand. "You know, I figured she would be older, certainly not someone as young as you."

"Actually I was adopted. My real parents were killed in a car accident soon after I was born. My mother was Margaret MacDonald's sister and the MacDonalds adopted me. They're the only parents I've known."

"When did you move to Glen Cairn?"

"After my parents died, about two years ago."

"I was sorry to hear about your loss. From everything I heard about them, your parents were exceptional people."

"They were. But if I had to lose them, I'm thankful they went together. They were so close. I'm not sure how one could have gone on without the other."

Greg remembered the attorney telling him something similar. It was a shame. He knew how senseless accidents happened, forever changing the lives of all involved.

He looked at his bowl and discovered it was empty. During their conversation he'd eaten everything she'd put in front of him. The pain in his chest had eased. When had that happened? He realized that he could breathe deeply without hurting. How long had he put up with the chest pains before he'd fallen sick? He couldn't remember.

Whatever Fiona had been doing for him had worked. He was embarrassed that he'd given her such a bad time. He could have been more gracious toward her.

"I—uh—want to thank you for caring for me," he finally said. "I know I haven't been a very good patient...."

"There's an understatement," she replied.

Greg noted she smiled when she said it. She had a beguiling smile. There were several rather intriguing things he'd noticed about her. He felt a strong tug of attraction and immediately squelched it.

"You're quite welcome, sir. Now, will you please tell me why you were looking for me? My curiosity isn't going to let me rest until I know." She poured them each a cup of tea and returned to her place at the table.

He looked at the cup. What he wouldn't give for a cup of coffee. He felt ungrateful after all she'd done, but tea was no substitute.

"I'm a private detective from New York," he began. "A client approached me several weeks ago and said she had recently discovered that she had been adopted. Since both of her adoptive parents are gone, she wants to find out who her birth parents were and something about her family tree. She hired me to investigate."

Fiona looked puzzled. "I'm sorry, but I'm not following you. What does that have to do with me?"

"James MacDonald was listed as the attending

physician on the birth certificate. I had the name of the solicitor who handled the adoption, Calvin McCloskey. It was Calvin who told me that the MacDonalds would be the only ones with more information, and both had died. When I heard they had a daughter, I decided to check out the only lead I'd found in Craigmor.''

''Calvin handled my parents' estates, despite the fact that he was retired,'' Fiona said. ''I don't know what I would have done without him.'' She paused as though thinking. Minutes passed in silence until she said, ''I can't imagine why my parents would have had anything to do with such an adoption, though. Craigmor has always been a close community. I never heard of anyone in the village giving up a child for adoption.''

''Yes, I've already run into that problem. I contacted Mr. McCloskey to discuss the matter. At first he showed no interest in discussing the matter with me, but at some point, thankfully, he changed his mind. Without his help I wouldn't have known where to continue my search.''

Fiona rested her arms on the table and leaned forward. ''This sounds like a good mystery. What did he tell you?''

''He said that your parents notified him that they had triplet girls whose mother died soon after giving birth. They told him that the only thing they knew was her first name, Moira, and that her husband, Douglas, had been murdered the night before by his brother. They contacted the solicitor for help in finding a safe home where they wouldn't be found. They came up with the idea to have them adopted separately.''

"How fascinating. When did this take place? You would think my parents would have spoken of such an unusual happening, but I never heard anything about triplets being born in Craigmor."

"My client's birth date is in my files. It was sometime late 1978."

"Oh!" she said with a chuckle. "No wonder I never heard talk about triplets. That was the year I was born. They had probably forgotten all about them by the time I was old enough to understand."

"You're twenty-five?" he asked, surprised.

"I will be next month. Why do you ask?"

"I thought you were in your teens. I had no idea…" He allowed his voice to trail off. After a moment of silence, he said, "I don't expect you to remember any of this, but I felt certain that someone in Craigmor might. However, everyone I asked insisted they had never heard of Moira and Douglas nor of triplets born in Craigmor."

"I can see your problem."

"I spoke to a couple of local doctors who knew your father. When I asked them for suggestions as to how I could proceed, one of them suggested I check with you."

"Why me?"

"Because you might know what happened to

your father's files. It's possible your father had a file on Moira and Douglas. I know it would be difficult to find them without a last name, but at this point, I have no other way to go. If I could check his files, I'm certain to come across the birth of triplets in that year, which would give me the parents' names. I feel badly that I have to go back to my client with the news that not only does she have sisters she never knew existed, but I lost the trail leading to her family once I discovered her parents are dead.''

Fiona nodded. ''Did Mr. McCloskey tell you who adopted the other girls? That might help in your search.''

''No. My questions were specific to my client and he was reluctant enough to give me what he did. He certainly wouldn't have divulged information about the other babies. He said his records contained nothing else about my client and I believe him.''

''And you think my father might have the information buried somewhere in his files?''

''I can only hope.''

''I'm not sure I can help you. For one thing, I don't have all of them. When I moved out of their home I removed all the files but didn't have room here to store everything. Most of my father's papers and files are at my aunt's home.''

Greg studied her in silence. ''Why did you move to Glen Cairn?''

"Craigmor had too many memories of my parents. I had to get away until I could deal with my grief. One of these days I'll probably go back. I haven't decided when."

"I guess what I'm asking is, why did you choose Glen Cairn?"

"The closest doctor to Glen Cairn is fifty-five miles away. When I learned that, I felt I could help the villagers if I came here. I believe I have."

Greg rubbed his forehead, feeling another headache beginning. What he was hearing was that there was a good chance she might not have the file he was searching for. For that matter, there might not *be* a file. There was a good likelihood that he would end up returning to New York without much more information than he had obtained when he'd first arrived in Scotland.

He tightened his jaw. Not if he could help it.

"Would you mind if I look through the files you have?" he asked.

"Not at all, but I need to warn you that it will take some time since you don't have a last name."

"Or…maybe I'll be lucky and find a file listed as an adoption. That would make my work considerably easier. In the meantime, I'll find a room in the village tonight and come back tomorrow to begin my search."

"There's no reason for you to find another place. As you can see, I have room for you to stay here."

He shook his head. "No, that won't do. You live alone. There's no reason to ruin your reputation by having me stay with you."

Her smile dazzled. "Too late."

He frowned. "What do you mean?"

"I had a visitor earlier today who discovered that you were here. By the time I went to the village, it was already an accepted fact that I was involved in an illicit and passionate love affair with a mystery man from who knows where."

His eyes narrowed. "I'm sorry. I'm responsible for crashing in on you like I did. I would have never believed I'd be sick for days before I came to my senses."

"Don't worry, I ignore the gossips and so should you. I do what I do without explanation. You were ill and needed a place to stay. Some people have little else to do than to speculate about other people's lives. So we'll let them."

He didn't say anything. Instead, he picked up his cup and drank, making a slight face.

"You don't care for the tea?"

"Oh. I'm sorry, I didn't mean to be rude. It's just that when I forget that what I'm drinking isn't coffee, the taste change catches me off guard."

"I can make you coffee, if you like."

"Really? I would be indebted to you more than I am now."

She hopped up from her chair and rummaged through one of her shelves. When she glanced around at him, she looked pleased with herself. "I knew I had some. I don't know how fresh it will be." She prepared a filter and the coffeemaker.

"Doesn't matter," he said. "If you don't mind my staying here, I'll take you up on your offer on the condition that you allow me to pay you."

She stopped measuring the coffee. "You're very determined, aren't you?"

"I wouldn't have it any other way, Ms. MacDonald."

"Please, call me Fiona. If you're going to continue to stay here, you don't need to be so formal."

"I'm Greg."

"Yes, I know."

"I mean, you may call me by that name, if you wish."

"Perhaps. We'll see." She started the coffee. "The files are in storage boxes in the garage. What I suggest is that you bring them in here to look through. There's no reason for you to create more congestion in your chest by working in an unheated storage room."

"So…you're okay with this?"

"Yes. I'm generally not home much in the daytime. There are several people whom I check in on every day. You'll have the place to yourself most of the time."

He nodded. "Thank you."

When the coffee stopped perking, she filled a

heavy mug with the dark liquid and handed it to him. "Do you need anything in it?"

"No. This is the way I like it." He sniffed the aroma circling up from the cup and sighed. "I've been having serious coffee withdrawal symptoms," he said. He carefully sipped the coffee and grinned. "Just the way I like it."

It was strong enough to curl the hair on his chest. He was used to drinking it that way from his years with the NYPD. Not that it had ever been this fresh. By the time he would pour a cup of coffee at the precinct, the stuff had been sitting in the pot for hours. His own office wasn't much better. This, he decided, was ambrosia.

A deep "woof" sound came from the other side of the door. Fiona let McTavish in. He entered with placid dignity and paused beside her. She rubbed his ears and Greg could have sworn the dog smiled. After a couple of minutes, McTavish ambled over to Greg's chair as though to greet him.

He scratched the mastiff's head. When he glanced up, Greg saw surprise on Fiona's face.

"What's wrong?" he asked.

"Nothing's wrong. I've never seen him quite this friendly to any of my visitors before. He's generally aloof with everyone but me." She looked at McTavish thoughtfully. "It's out of character."

"On the contrary, it's obvious he's a great judge of character, aren't you, fella?"

"I can tell that you're feeling much better this evening."

"Why not? I must have slept through the past several days. It's a wonder I don't have bed sores," he added with a grin.

"Do you have a fever?"

He shrugged. "I doubt it. I'm feeling very close to my normal self."

"Why don't we go into the front room so I can start the fire?" she asked, transferring their dishes to the sink. When she turned, she saw that Greg had already left the room. She went looking for him and found him in the living room, kneeling in front of the fireplace. When he turned and looked at her, he was frowning. "Did you lose something?" she asked.

"I was looking for your wood so I could start a fire."

"Ahh. Then you'll have a long search, I'm afraid. I use peat to heat the place. Wood is at a premium here."

He stepped away and allowed Fiona access to the fireplace. He walked to the wingback chair, sat down and watched her. When she finished, she set the screen in front of the fire and took her place in the chair across from him.

Tiger leaped into her lap and stood staring at her. She obligingly spread the lap robe over her and waited until he curled up into a ball on top of it.

"What's your cat's name?" he asked.

"Tiger."

"Makes sense."

"He was but a wee kitten when I discovered him by my back door. I don't doubt one of the children from the village placed him there, knowing I wouldn't be able to turn him away. Of course everyone I asked had absolutely no idea what I was talking about."

"Do you get lonely living so isolated?"

"You would think so, wouldn't you? However, my days are full, what with caring for the adults and helping some of the mothers with their sick children."

"Ah, now I understand."

"What do you understand?"

He grinned. "Your bedside manner. It explains why you were treating me like a child."

"Not at all. I was merely responding to your childish behavior," she promptly responded, causing him to laugh. Because he seemed to be in a better frame of mind, she asked, "I know that it isn't any of my business, but I was wondering if you'd share a little something about yourself with me."

"Why?" he asked bluntly.

He'd tensed and she felt sad that he could be so threatened by such an innocent question. "Perhaps so that we might get to know each other a little better. You've found out a great many things about me—where I live, my pets, what I do with my time, even my age. I know nothing about you except that you're a private investigator. I was wondering why you chose that profession, as an example, and what your family is like. That sort of thing.''

He stared at her for what seemed like a long time before he said, ''Perhaps it would be better if I found another place to stay after all. I would prefer to keep our relationship strictly on a professional level.''

Chapter Five

Fiona sat staring at the flickering flames in the fireplace long after Greg had left the living room. McTavish and Tiger kept her company. She knew it was late and she needed to go to bed and catch up on her rest, and yet she continued to sit while her thoughts tumbled around in her head.

Despite her assurance to Greg that she would not pry into his personal life if that was his wish, Greg had immediately returned to his room.

She continued to ponder his behavior. No doubt he was right. He was a professional doing his job. He was not interested in her other than to have access to her father's files. Her interest in him was beyond good taste, and he had reminded her of that in no uncertain terms.

He had logically defined their situation. He would do what he needed to do, then go his own way. She would not disturb him with intrusive questions.

She'd been wrestling with the same or similar thoughts for hours. Her problem was she couldn't seem to put Greg and his emotional pain out of her mind. He carried such hurt in so many areas that had nothing to do with his illness. He was still recovering, yet through sheer force of will he refused to admit to weakness of any kind.

Not long after leaving her, Greg's cough returned. She'd made more tea and took it to him. When she reached his door, she tapped lightly and waited.

She heard him stirring. When he opened the door, his unbuttoned shirt hung open. She forced herself to look him in the eye. "I made you tea for your cough. I thought you might want to keep it in your room."

He glanced at the tray in her hand, then at her, before he took the tray from her. "Thanks," he said gruffly, sounding hoarse.

"If you wish to sleep with your chest covered, please help yourself to the shirts in the second drawer of the dresser."

"Whose shirts are they?"

"My father's. I sometimes sleep in them myself. They're very comfortable.

Fiona turned away.

"Wait," he said.

She turned around. "Yes?"

"I didn't mean to offend you earlier."

"Nor did I mean to offend you. I was out of line."

"No, actually you weren't. It's my problem. I don't talk about my past."

"Nor should you be expected to."

He nodded. "Thank you for the tea. I really appreciate it."

"You're welcome."

She'd waited until he closed the door before she'd returned to the living room. Now she sat and mulled over what she had learned about Greg Dumas. She didn't need to hear what had caused his pain. Her only desire was to assist in easing it. If he felt his past was too painful to discuss, it would continue to fester within him, causing him mental, emotional and physical problems.

For a while she had tried to read, only to discover that the intriguing novel she'd been absorbed in when Greg had arrived on her doorstep could no longer hold her attention. Life had impinged on her quiet time.

Fiona didn't know what she could do, if anything, to help him. She had done what she could for his physical pain. She never worked with a person on an emotional level without gaining permission. It was obvious that Greg had no intention of granting it.

In general, Fiona stayed detached from those who came to her for help in healing. Otherwise, she would be too drained of energy to be of assistance to anyone.

She knew that this time, staying detached where Greg was concerned would be a challenge. No matter how much she reasoned with herself, she was attracted to him, more attracted than she'd been to any man she'd ever met. Schoolgirl crushes and casual friendships during her teen years had gone nowhere. She'd understood that most males found her strange abilities off-putting. Greg's reaction to her herbal teas had been typical. Most men were wary of unfamiliar things.

Greg was more than wary. He had an emotional wall built around him so thick, she doubted if anyone could reach him. She wondered if the Jill he'd mentioned had anything to do with his walls? Had she hurt him in some way that he'd been unable to forgive?

Her heart ached in response to his pain, a reliable sign that she was not detached. *This must stop,* she thought. *He will be gone in a few days, disappearing from my life as suddenly as he'd appeared.*

Fiona banked the fire, turned off the light and went upstairs. Tiger and McTavish followed. Once in bed Fiona focused her mind on a soothing meditation that helped when she had difficulty relaxing.

Tiger hopped up on the bed and curled into a ball at her feet. McTavish stretched out on the braided rug beside her bed. With a sigh of unnamed regret, Fiona closed her eyes.

Breakfast was ready when Greg walked into the kitchen the next morning. The first Fiona was aware of his presence was when he said, "I smelled the coffee. It was enough to bring me out of a deep sleep."

She turned away from the toaster and looked at him. He'd splashed water on his face and combed his hair, although his cheeks were rough with an overnight stubble.

He was dressed in jeans and a sweater, an ordinary choice. So why was her heart thumping so?

"Good morning," she said without smiling. "How are you feeling?"

"Better than I have in a long while. My chest no longer hurts. My head is clear and I'm ready to get to work."

She nodded and set a plate filled with food at his place. "Then eat and I'll show you where the files are stored." She poured the coffee and set the cup next to his plate.

He needed no second invitation. As soon as he was seated, Greg picked up the coffee, sniffed the aroma and smiled with pleasure before sipping the hot brew.

"Thank you," he said when he replaced his cup with a pleased sigh.

You would think I'd given him the keys to the richest kingdom around, she thought.

"You're welcome." She sat across from him and began to eat.

After the silence between them lengthened, Greg said, "I meant what I said to you last night. I sincerely hope I didn't offend you."

"I understand that you're a very private person and I respect that."

He gave his head a quick shake of disagreement. "I've never been good about talking about myself."

"Few people are, you know."

He chuckled. "I can cite a half-dozen people I know who would prove that theory wrong."

She finished her breakfast, picked up her plate and placed it in the sink full of sudsy water. A short time later she felt his presence and glanced around. He stood nearby with his plate. She took it from him. "Thank you."

Instead of moving away, he leaned against the counter and crossed his arms. "You're a very good cook. Has anyone ever told you?" he asked in a conversational tone. She would almost consider his mood to be expansive this morning.

"Thank you again," she said, feeling a little flustered. "I love to eat, you see."

His gaze traveled from her sweater-clad shoulders to her heavy cotton pants and ankle-high boots. "You don't look as if you carry an extra ounce of weight anywhere."

She fought the heated flush that enveloped her and, as always, lost the battle. She lamented having such fair skin. She had no way to hide her embarrassment. Fiona concentrated on washing the dishes.

"You're close to rubbing the flowers off that plate, you know," he said. She could hear the amusement in his voice. Her cheeks felt as though they were on fire.

She hastily rinsed the plate and placed it in the dish drainer. Quickly drying her hands, she said, "Let me show you the storage room," without looking at him. She grabbed the key ring off the hook and went to the back door. Without looking to see if he followed, Fiona stepped outside.

The wind whipped around her, blowing her loose hair into a frenzy of tangles. She ignored it, striding along the path that went through her herb garden. She unlocked the garage and went inside. She headed to the storage room in back and opened the door.

She heard Greg behind her. Without turning, she said, "As you can see, there is no electricity out here. I would suggest you bring the boxes into the house.'' She turned and faced him. ''Here are the keys. I will be gone most of today. Mrs. Tabor is having some difficulties with the early stages of her pregnancy. I promised her I would come visit and answer any questions she might have, since this is her first child. I don't know how long I'll be gone.''

He held out his hand and she dropped the keys into it.

Without waiting for a possible reply, she stepped around him and left the building. She felt that the hounds of hell were nipping at her heels. She did not want to encourage his friendliness. She was much too susceptible to him *without* seeing his charming side.

There had been times when she'd been convinced he *had* no charming side. Leave it to Greg to prove her wrong.

He watched her leave, wishing—not for the first time—that he hadn't reacted so strongly to her questions the night before. At the very least, he could have been a little more diplomatic. He knew he had offended her and his rudeness was inexcusable, regardless of his apology.

Fiona was the first woman he'd noticed, really registered seeing, since he'd lost Jill. By the time he woke up this morning, he'd stopped kidding himself that he wasn't affected by her. He'd been dreaming about her, which had unnerved him. He'd pushed the dream out of his mind, or thought he had, until he'd walked into the kitchen and saw her standing there.

His body had reacted instantly, wanting to reenact the erotic dreams he'd had the night before. He'd been startled by the unexpected response. He'd had no desire to make love to a woman since Jill had died. He'd figured there would never be another woman who attracted him in that way. Now he knew he was wrong. The problem was that he didn't know what to do about his reaction to her. He was a guest in her home, although he fully intended to pay her for his stay. Nevertheless he did not want to take advantage of her.

He had finally managed to overcome his instant physical response to her by concentrating on his gratitude for all she had done for him. Not only had she taken him in, she had known what to do to help him recover from his illness.

Once awake this morning, Greg realized that he felt better than he had in months and he'd wanted to thank her for all she'd done, but one look at her face when she turned and saw him in the kitchen warned him that she wouldn't be interested in hearing anything he had to say.

He deserved her cool reception—thanks to his blasted moods—but he already missed her friendliness, her stern lectures about his health, her adorable smile.

Greg forced himself to look around the dim room. The garage door kept slapping against the wall with each wind gust. With the way the heavy clouds were scudding through the sky, he wouldn't be surprised if the area would be drenched in the near future.

He turned back to the boxes. Not one of them was marked. Of course he wouldn't know what to look for if a box *was* marked, except for dates. That probably wouldn't work. A doctor might keep a patient's file for years. Surely there was a file in all these boxes for a Douglas and Moira who'd had triplets. It was strange, though, how everyone he spoke to in Craigmor was adamant about never hearing of triplets or a couple named Moira and Douglas.

Well, standing there looking at the stack of boxes wasn't going to get him any further in his quest. With new determination, Greg picked up two of the boxes and carried them into the house with him.

McTavish greeted him at the kitchen door.

Greg didn't know how, but he knew that Fiona was gone. She hadn't taken her car because it was in the garage. He wondered how far it was to Glen Cairn. He might drive there to see.

He strode down the hall and paused in the archway of the living room. She'd already built a fire there. He might as well take advantage of it. He placed the boxes on the floor and went back outside. Two more trips gave him more than enough

to look through in a day. His last venture outside
was to relock the garage.

The sky spit drops of moisture as he left the
garage. He wasted no time returning to the warmth
of Fiona's home. No reason to become ill again.
After this week, he'd had enough of that to last the
rest of his life. But what about Fiona? He hoped
she'd worn something waterproof.

"Ah, Fiona," Timothy McGregor said when she
entered the greengrocer's shop. His beaming smile
and dancing eyes sparkled in his round face. "I've
been missin' that lovely smile of yours. I hope you
haven't been ill."

"Never, Timmy," she replied to the almost-bald
man twice her age. "I have been busy, though. I'm
certain you've heard about my guest as well as the
number of calls I've been getting from families
who have someone ill in their homes. I hope this
isn't going to be too harsh a winter. Too many
villagers have weakened immune systems going
into the season, what with one ailment or another
popping up."

She picked out some fresh vegetables while she
spoke.

"Well, as to your visitor, I've heard so many
stories, I've been forced to discount each and every
one," he said, his eyes twinkling. "Some say he's
your long-lost brother, or cousin or some other
type of relative. Others are convinced he's the rea-

son you've refused to go out with any of our local lads and that you've been engaged to him for a couple of years or more.''

She shook her head in wonder. ''Amazing, isn't it? Despite the lack of a single fact upon which to base suppositions, the stories mushroom anyway.''

''So who *is* your visitor, if I may ask?''

''His name is Greg Dumas and he's looking through some of my father's files hoping to locate some information for a client in the States.''

''You don't say? Who is he looking for?''

''That's one of his problems. He doesn't know. Somehow he managed to trace the adoption of triplets to my father, but he doesn't have a last name for the birth parents. It seems to me that the birth of triplets is enough of an oddity that my father would have mentioned such an occurrence, but I've never heard about them. I showed Mr. Dumas the boxes of files I have in storage and left him to his hunt.''

''How long does he intend to stay?''

''Until he finds a file giving more information on the parents, I suppose.''

''Be careful that you don't have a permanent resident there once he becomes accustomed to your cooking and baking.''

She laughed as he'd meant for her to. ''I'll be careful. Perhaps I'll overcook a dish from time to time. That should discourage him.''

When she left the shop, she was smiling. Timothy had been one of the first people she'd met when she first visited there. He'd understood without her saying that her grief was much too deep to discuss. He'd steered her to the realty office when she mentioned rental property, and from there she had found her snug cottage. In the two years since she'd moved to Glen Cairn, she'd slowly come to terms with the unexpected loss of her parents.

She hadn't been ready to let them go, but then, who is ever ready?

Perhaps that was why Greg refused to talk about his past. He may have suffered a grievous loss too painful to discuss. She intended to honor his reticence and ask no more questions, despite her embarrassingly strong curiosity to learn everything there was to know about him.

After visiting Mrs. Tabor and checking on several other villagers, Fiona returned home carrying her umbrella. There had been rain earlier in the day, but now the sky had cleared. It looked as if there was going to be a beautiful sunset.

She paused on her walk home to gaze at the vista of rolling hills and glints of water that were so much a part of the western Highlands. All else considered, she had chosen a lovely place in which to deal with her grief.

Fiona gave a sigh of contentment and continued on her way. For her noon meal, she'd eaten some fruit, homemade bread given to her by the mother of one of her patients and some cheese. Now she was ready for a hot meal.

Would Greg have known to look for food in her kitchen? She'd neglected to tell him to help himself to whatever he found. Well, if he weren't willing to search for food, it would be his own fault if he went hungry.

Light had faded from the sky by the time she reached home and saw a gleaming lamp beckoning through the front window. Fiona found it unexpectedly charming to come home to a lighted window and to someone with whom to visit before bedtime.

She had a flash of what it might be like not to go to her bed alone. With that thought came the sudden flood of emotions that swept over her every time she thought about the brief intimacy she'd shared with Greg. That night had awakened her to another world, one of sensuous pleasure. She would never be the same again.

Stop mooning over a stranger you can't have and think about what you're going to prepare for dinner, she scolded herself.

Greg took a break from his search about midafternoon. He hadn't wanted to overlook something, so he had carefully read enough data from each file to know it wasn't the one he was searching for.

He'd made more coffee midmorning, and at noon he'd found the ingredients for a sandwich.

Now he stopped and warmed the coffee. Once it was ready, he returned to the living room and glanced at the time. It was close to eight o'clock in Queens. Tina would be almost ready for bed.

He hadn't spoken to her in almost a week and decided it was past time for him to call her. He used his calling card and soon heard Helen and George Santini's phone ringing.

Helen answered on the third ring.

"Hope I'm not interrupting anything," Greg said.

"Greg! Oh, it's wonderful to hear your voice. Hold on, will you?"

He listened as she called to Tina. "Tina! Your daddy's on the phone." She spoke into the phone. "I'm sorry to do this at the beginning of the call, but she has been pestering me for several days, wondering when you'll be home."

"Daddy, Daddy, Daddy!" Tina's voice bounced through the phone. "When are you coming home, Daddy? I miss you! And I have lots and lots to tell you!"

"You do, huh? Then why don't you tell me now?"

"Oh. Well, I got to wear a new dress to school today because they took our pictures."

"They did? How come I didn't know about it?"

"'Cause they only told us like maybe yesterday. Or sometime like that."

He heard Helen say, "The teacher sent a note home last Friday."

"Yeah," Tina said, "on Friday."

"What kind of dress did you wear?"

"A beeootiful one. Gramma picked it out for me. It's got red and green in it."

"A plaid," Helen said in the background.

"A plaid," Tina dutifully repeated. "Gramma said it's the kind they wear where you are."

"Ah, a Scottish plaid. I can hardly wait to see it."

"Gramma took pictures when I was ready to go to school so you can see them when you come home. When are you coming home, Daddy? You've been gone for weeks and weeks."

He rubbed the frown lines between his eyebrows. "Honey, I really don't know. Daddy's looking for something for a client. I need to stay here until I find it."

"Oh." After a brief pause, she said, "But you said it would only take a few days and it's been longer than a few, Daddy. It's been a loooooong time!"

"I know, baby. It's been a long time for me, too." He cleared his throat. "It's time for you to go to bed now, isn't it?"

"Uh-huh. Granpa said he'd read me a story like you do."

"Good for Granpa. I love you, sweetheart. Why don't you let me talk to Gramma now?"

When Helen came back on the line, he said, "I'm sorry this is taking longer than expected."

"Oh, Greg. I know you'd be here if you could. She's been very good, except for getting a note from her teacher about talking in class, but that doesn't surprise any of us who know her."

They both chuckled at the thought of Tina, the magpie, being quiet in class.

"How's your case going?" Helen asked.

"To be honest, I'm becoming more and more discouraged. After that first run of luck getting information from the solicitor, I thought I'd have my answers in a few days. As you know, it hasn't turned out that way.

"I went to Craigmor in hope of finding a relative of the doctor involved with the adoption."

"And you didn't find anyone? Oh, dear. That *is* unfortunate."

"Well, I did find his daughter, but she's too young to know anything about it."

"What do you intend to do?"

"I'm at the daughter's home at the moment. She no longer lives in Craigmor so it took me time to find her. Then I picked up some kind of bug that laid me low. At least the daughter had something to help me overcome whatever it was."

"How fortunate. She's a doctor, too, then?"

"I don't know much about her credentials. All I know is whatever she did worked wonders on me."

"I'm sorry to hear you succumbed to something. You've been driving yourself much too hard, you know. Thank goodness you found someone who was able to help you."

"Amen to that."

"Well, don't you worry about anything here. We're doing fine...and I know you'll find what you're looking for before long. You don't discourage easily."

He laughed. "So you told me when you tried to convince me I wasn't the right person to marry Jill."

"Of course, you enjoy bringing that up, don't you? Just to hear me admit I was wrong about you."

He sobered. "Actually, you weren't wrong, Helen. If she hadn't married me, she'd still be alive today. We should have listened to you."

"You know that isn't true. You can't control every criminal who breaks the law in the city, Greg."

"I wish I'd thought of that sooner."

"Please stop beating up on yourself over what can't be changed. At least we have Tina, who, by the way, has one more thing she needs to tell you before she goes to bed."

"Okay, but first I want you to take this phone number down in case you need to reach me. I'll try to do better about checking in with you."

Once Greg recited the number, Helen handed the

phone to Tina who was filled with more news about school, and her kitten and the plans being made for the weekend. When she finally ran down, he said, ''Daddy really misses you, baby girl. Pretend I'm there to give you a big hug and a smooch, okay?''

Fiona hadn't meant to eavesdrop. She'd come in through the kitchen to put the vegetables away when she'd heard Greg's voice. She thought someone was there with him. She stopped in the hallway when she heard him say something about marrying Jill and that she would be alive today if it hadn't been for him. After hearing that, she could not force herself to walk away.

When she heard him say that he missed his daughter, she understood the enormity of the burden Greg carried.

Chapter Six

Fiona was embarrassed that she had stooped to eavesdropping in order to discover more about Greg. He had no reason to believe that anyone was there besides himself. She should have slammed a door or something to announce her arrival.

Unfortunately it was too late for any of that. Now she would have to live with what she had inadvertently discovered.

Fiona hurriedly prepared a nourishing meal. When it was ready she went back down the hallway and paused in the archway of the living room. "I've made something to eat, if you're hungry," she said.

Greg looked startled. "Oh. Hi. I didn't hear you come in."

She took a deep breath. "I came in while you were on the phone. I would have said something then but didn't want to disturb your conversation."

He gazed at her without smiling.

"Are you hungry?" she asked.

He stood and dusted his hands. "You bet. Even though I found the pound cake and ate a large slice of that with coffee this afternoon. Hope you don't mind that I made another pot. Coffee keeps my heart pumping."

"Not at all. I forgot to mention that you were to treat the kitchen as your own while you're here."

"Your kitchen is nothing like mine. I rarely have anything but milk and breakfast food on hand. The rest of my shopping is in the frozen-food department." He paused in the archway and looked down at her. "Let me go wash some of this dust off and I'll be ready."

Fiona couldn't meet his eyes. "All right," she replied, and returned to the kitchen. She leaned against the counter and closed her eyes. She was in deep trouble and didn't know what to do about it. No doubt she was more susceptible because she had never been in such an intimate situation with a man before. Their routine must be similar to how a married couple lives.

She hadn't realized how much she'd missed

Greg today until she saw him again. It was then her emotions came tumbling out of some secret place she never knew existed.

It didn't help that he looked at her in a more intimate way than he had at first. He'd been sick, of course. Now he wasn't. She could not ignore that he was the same man who had nuzzled her neck and fondled her breast, thinking she was his dead wife.

The only way she could face him was to remind herself that he didn't remember that night. Her problem was that she did. She couldn't force what had happened out of her mind. She kept reliving what she had felt when he'd touched her and stroked her and—God help her—she wanted to feel those emotions again.

"Mmm, something smells good," Greg said, walking into the kitchen. She immediately straightened but it was too late. "Is there something wrong?" he asked.

She shook her head. "I'm just tired, that's all." She motioned for him to be seated, then sat down across from him. "How was your day? Did you have any luck finding what you're looking for?"

"Well, let's put it this way. I've eliminated a great many files that don't contain what I'm looking for," Greg said. "Is there anyone in your family who might remember something that happened twenty-five years ago?"

She thought for a moment. "Actually, there is.

My aunt, Minnie MacDonald, was born in Craigmor. She will no doubt die there. I would guess that she knows everyone who's lived there since she was born. She's the one who has the rest of dad's files.''

"I wonder why no one mentioned her when I was asking for information?''

She laughed. "They were trying to protect you, I'm sure.''

"From what?''

"Aunt Minnie has a very sharp tongue and very little patience with anyone. I doubt that she would have told a stranger anything. She's a little independent.''

He widened his eyes deliberately. "An independent MacDonald. I can't imagine it.'' Then he smiled, a slow, intimate smile that created a familiar flutter in her midsection. Oh, yes, this man's presence was definitely lethal to her peace of mind.

"If you would like, I could take you to see her if you don't find what you're looking for here. She might be more forthcoming if I'm there.''

He shook his head. "I can't take you away from your own work. You've done more than enough for me this past week.''

She smiled. "Just part of the service, sir. Helping to return a person to optimum health is what I do.''

"You do it very well,'' he said quietly.

"Thank you.'' She met his eyes and was startled

at the warmth in them. He'd not looked at her with that expression before. It was filled with admiration and something more. The something more made her nervous. Had he discovered how strongly she was drawn to him? Oh, she hoped not. That would be much too embarrassing to be borne.

"Well, let's see how my search goes. I may not have a choice except to meet with your aunt. I'm rapidly running out of options."

Once they finished eating, Greg excused himself and returned to work. Fiona cleaned up the kitchen and tried to think of something she could do that wouldn't involve following him into the living room.

She was being silly, she admonished herself. What she was experiencing was merely a delayed adolescent infatuation. She'd missed that part of growing up and she needed to learn to deal with it.

There was no time like the present.

With that in mind, Fiona went to the living room and curled up in her chair with her book. From time to time she glanced at Greg, who was using her desk to sort through files. From the way the boxes were arranged, he must have gone through six of them today, with two more waiting to be opened.

Once she began to read, the magic of the written word swept her into the story and she no longer noticed her surroundings.

McTavish was in his favorite place, on the rug in front of the fireplace. Tiger sat on the arm of her chair, dozing. When she glanced up, she realized that sleet was pinging against the windows.

She glanced at Greg and discovered that he was relaxed back in the chair at her desk watching her. From his comfortable position, it looked as though he'd been doing so for a while.

Her cheeks immediately heated up.

"Why do you do that?" he asked.

"Do what?"

"Blush every time you find me looking at you?"

She swallowed, wishing she could think of some lighthearted reply. The truth was, she didn't have much experience in that field...which she finally decided was the only answer she could offer.

"I'm not used to being watched," she admitted, rubbing her cheek in a vain attempt to hide her discomfort.

"Are all the men around here blind?"

"I don't know what you mean."

"Hasn't anyone ever told you what a beautiful woman you are, Fiona? What's more important is that your beauty comes from inside, as well."

She closed her eyes, too flustered to attempt a reply of any sort.

"I'm not trying to embarrass you, you know," he said softly from his position across the room from her.

"You don't have to try, it seems. You said you aren't used to talking about yourself. Well, I'm not used to having attention on me, either. I find it uncomfortable."

"I'm not a very interesting subject."

"There's no reason for us to become better acquainted." Fiona picked up her book and resumed reading, although she had no idea what the words meant. She was too aware of the man across the room. She was concentrating so hard on ignoring him that when he spoke she jumped.

"I used to work for the New York Police Department until three years ago when I resigned and opened my own investigation agency. That pretty much sums up my life."

She thought about his wife, Jill, who he felt died because of him, and his daughter, whom he obviously loved very much.

Fiona nodded. "I apologize for pushing to learn more about you," she said once again. "If you'll excuse me, I need to get ready for bed." What she needed was to get away from this man. Whether he mentioned them or not, she was aware of the strong emotions he held firmly in check. At the moment, all she wanted to do was to draw him into her arms and assure him that he was all right.

He would never believe it, of course. She had no reason to believe that what she felt was true. All she knew was that this man affected her as no other had.

She walked past him on her way to the door and he stopped her by touching her arm. When she looked up at him inquiringly, he said, "There is something about me that you need to know, though."

Fiona stepped away from his touch. "And that is?"

"I'm very attracted to you, which is unusual for me. I guess the reason I'm telling you is that I want to reassure you that I would never take advantage of this situation. You have nothing to fear from me."

His eyes reflected what he said with such clarity that she hadn't needed to hear the words. Except that she did.

"My confession has obviously struck you speechless, which makes me feel more of a fool than ever," Greg said with a hint of irritation. "I shouldn't have mentioned it."

"It isn't that, Greg," she whispered. "What unnerves me is the fact that I'm attracted to you, as well."

Chapter Seven

His eyes darkened with a surge of what Fiona
guessed was lust, which was understandable given
the circumstances. She felt the same thing at the
moment and wondered if her expression mirrored
her feelings. For the first time in her life, Fiona
wanted to become intimate with a man—with this
man. She wanted to touch and explore him without
interruption. She wanted to feel his heart beat beneath her palm. She wanted to become one with
him.

Her mouth went dry at the thought.

He closed his eyes briefly before saying, "I wish
you hadn't said that." His voice reflected pained

amusement. "On that note, I think I'd better say good-night, as well."

She could see his bedroom door through the archway and watched as he stopped with his hand on the doorknob. He looked back at her. "Of course I wouldn't be taking advantage of the situation if you decided to kiss me, would I?"

Fiona heard the words and her body immediately responded. She felt disconnected from her body, confused by all that she was feeling, while her body knew exactly what she wanted. As though she'd lost her will to resist, she walked toward him, stopping inches away from his chest.

He cupped her face in his palms. "This isn't a good idea and we both know it. I don't want to hurt you in any way."

Several thoughts swirled in her head at his words. She knew that although he wanted her on a physical level, he was irritated by the attraction. Common sense told her that she was foolish to linger there in the hall with him, and yet all she wanted to do was wrap herself around his warmth.

"I'm fairly sturdy, you know," she managed to say over the lump in her throat.

His eyes filled with amusement before his mouth curved into a smile. "*Sturdy* isn't the first word that comes to mind whenever I think of you...or when I dream of you, which seems to be happening with alarming frequency."

The lump in her throat blocked anything else she

might have said. It was just as well that he didn't wait for a response. Instead, he leaned down and, with a gentleness she would never have expected from this man, brushed his lips lightly across her mouth as though to accustom her to his touch.

Her eyelids fluttered closed and she allowed herself just to feel. All thoughts were released into the ether as she gave in to sensation. He brushed the tip of his tongue along the line of her mouth, as though he wanted something from her.

She sighed, her lips opening slightly. He oh-so-delicately skimmed his mouth over hers, settling against her until she felt the bold ridge of his erection.

She didn't pull away, although he was in no way restraining her. Instead, she moved into him, silently signaling that she didn't want the kiss to end. Not just yet, please.

He shifted his hands slightly, carefully, until he touched both her shoulders. She went up on tiptoe, wanting something more without knowing what it was, until he slipped his tongue inside. She knew now she was in deep trouble because she wanted more, so much more, and knew it would be beyond foolish for her to continue.

With all the strength she could muster, Fiona stepped back, breathing hard, her hands clenched at her sides. Only then did she realize that she hadn't touched him at all—at least not with her hands. Then again, she felt as though through their shared kiss, she had somehow touched his soul…as he had hers.

"I—uh—have to let McTavish outside now," she said breathlessly.

Greg nodded solemnly, only his eyes betraying his amusement. "Of course you do," he agreed in a soothing voice. "Good night, Fiona. Sleep well." He turned and went into his room, quietly closing the door behind him.

McTavish, having heard his name, joined her in the hallway. She rested her hand on his shoulder and relied on his strength to aid her in navigating the hall. They walked together to the back door, which she opened. McTavish leaped out as though he'd been caged for most of the day. She knew better because he'd had a nice long run after he ate earlier.

Fiona stepped outside with him, allowing the cold night air to cool her blood. The sleet had turned into a heavy mist. She walked to the bench that overlooked her herb garden and sat, staring blindly into the distance.

She felt as though she were a speeding train out of control and nearing a washed-out bridge. She needed to put on her brakes but wasn't at all certain they would hold if she spent much more time with Greg.

She'd never met anyone like him, which wasn't saying much, really. Her choice to distance herself from others had kept her more isolated than she'd realized until Greg arrived. Instead of feeling hemmed in by having to share her home, she'd discovered that she enjoyed his company.

Would she be able to return to her usual routine once he left, without feeling as though there was something lacking in her life?

McTavish appeared out of the night and placed his head on her thigh. "Hi, fellow," she said. "Are you ready to go to bed?"

She'd used the magic word and he immediately trotted to the back door. It wasn't that he cared one way or the other about bed, since he slept whenever he felt like it. However, he knew that at bedtime he received a special doggie treat.

As soon as she opened the door, he charged in ahead of her and slid to a stop in front of the pantry door. She shook her head at how easy it was to please a dog. Much easier than pleasing a person…a man. She had no experience in that area and wouldn't know how to begin.

Why was she thinking about it? There could be no relationship with Greg. He had a family and a job in the States and he was eager to return home. At most, he might find her an amusing distraction while he was in Scotland. As for Fiona, she wasn't at all certain she could be a distraction of any kind, amusing or not.

She gave McTavish his treat, made certain everything was locked up and the fire tended for the night and went upstairs. She sincerely hoped she could sleep. If she didn't want a repeat of these confusing feelings every time she was around Greg, she had better plan her schedule for the next couple of days so that she was away from home most of the time.

Surely he would have ended his search by then and moved on.

She could only hope.

"Good morning," Greg said, walking into the kitchen the next day.

He looked rested. Well, bully for him, she thought, silently pouring his coffee. She had tossed and turned all night, unable to relax. The little sleep she managed was filled with dreams of Greg. Of course her dreams were a little vague as to what actually happened, but she had definitely felt the heightened emotions he provoked within her, exactly what she hadn't wanted to experience.

"Did you sleep all right?" he asked, his voice carrying a note of concern. He'd probably noticed the dark circles beneath her eyes...another mark against her fair skin.

She gave him a quick glance. "Just fine." She set a plate piled high with food in front of him before returning to the sink where she washed up the utensils she'd used.

"Aren't you going to eat?" he asked.

"I've already eaten, thank you," she said without turning around. "I need to be in town early this morning, I don't know when I'll be back."

"Before you leave, there's something I need to ask you."

She closed her eyes, stifled a sigh and carefully dried her hands before she turned and faced him.

Oh, my, yes, he looked exceedingly virile this morning; there was no getting around it. The silver gray of his heavy knit sweater matched his eyes…as though he needed anything to call attention to them.

"Yes?"

"Ever since you mentioned your aunt, I've been thinking. Rather than continue going through the files you have, I believe I might save time by discussing my search with her. Who knows? Maybe she knows something about Moira and Douglas. If so, she could very well be the answer to my search." He picked up his fork and began to eat.

Fiona thought about it. He was right. That would be a workable plan. Plus it had the added bonus of removing him from her home. The trick would be to get Aunt Minnie to cooperate. She didn't leave her house much. More than that, she didn't care for strangers. Fiona had a hunch that Greg would be quite a shock to Aunt Minnie's system.

"What do you think?"

She crossed her arms and leaned against the counter. "Aunt Minnie knows everybody. If your client was born in Craigmor, I'm sure that Aunt

Minnie would know her parents. The trick will be to get her to discuss them with you.''

He nodded as he finished a piece of toast. ''I know. I ran into the same lack of response when I was in Craigmor asking questions. You Scots are a suspicious group, all right,'' he said lightly.

She could not resist returning his smile. ''If you think the townspeople are suspicious, they're chatterboxes compared to Aunt Minnie. She's the keeper of many secrets and is known for being very closemouthed.''

''Do you think she might talk to me if you go with me?''

She felt a sinking feeling deep in her stomach. ''Me?''

''Yes. You mentioned earlier that you would be willing to introduce us and let her know that I'm harmless so that she'll be willing to cooperate.''

She'd forgotten she'd made the suggestion. What had she been thinking? ''I did, didn't I?'' she replied with dismay.

''Then you'll go with me?'' he asked.

After a moment, she said, ''I don't think it's a good idea for me to go. I have so much to do and I...'' She stopped, hearing herself blather. She frowned and picked up his plate, turning toward the sink.

Greg stood. ''You certainly got up on the wrong side of the bed this morning, didn't you? Why the attitude change? What's wrong with my suggestion?''

She stood convicted but refused to give him the pleasure of admitting it. "After giving the matter more thought, I don't think my going with you is necessary. A phone call telling her about you would serve the same purpose. I can call and explain that you want to meet with her. After that, you're on your own."

"You don't like her?" he guessed.

"I adore her."

"Then what's the problem?"

I'll be cooped up in an automobile with you for four hours if I go with you. She couldn't tell him that, of course. But what other excuse did she have? She'd taken a few days off from time to time and the people around Glen Cairn had managed to survive just fine without her.

She turned away from the sink and looked at him. How honest did she want to be with him? She gazed into his mesmerizing eyes.

Not very.

In a conscious effort to sound offhand, she said, "You just caught me unprepared, that's all. If you think I will be of help in your investigation, of course I'll go with you."

"Good," he said, stepping away from the table. She hoped he didn't intend to come any closer. Right now the table was between them. She wasn't sure whom the table was protecting at the moment, but she didn't want to delve into that particular subject, either. "When can you leave?" he asked.

"Not before noon or thereabouts. I have several people to see today."

He nodded. "All right. While you're gone I'll continue looking through files. Who knows? I may find just what I'm looking for and I won't have to drag you away from your duties."

Was he making fun of her? she wondered. She stared at him but all she saw was an awareness…of her. The prospect of spending several hours in the car with her didn't appear to trouble him, while all she wanted to do was to stay as far away from him as possible.

"Well," she said briskly, "I must go. I'll be back as quickly as possible. We don't want to be on the road after dark, if we can avoid it." She went out and closed the door.

Greg placed his hands in his back pockets and rocked back on his heels, staring at the door. McTavish walked over to the door and sniffed, then turned to look at Greg.

"Wonder what put me on her snit list? You have any idea?"

McTavish wagged his tail in a sympathetic gesture and walked over to Greg. Greg scratched his ears. "I'll bring in some more boxes. Who knows? Maybe I'll find something and be out of her hair by nightfall. From her attitude, that would please her the most."

* * *

He stopped midmorning and made more coffee. He glanced at his watch. Tina would be home from school by now.

He called and chatted with Tina and Helen, gave them an update on his plans. When he was ready to end the conversation, he said to Helen, "If this trip back to Craigmor doesn't turn up new information, I'm going to head home. I've checked out every lead I could find. I have a hunch the people in the village know something and could help, but no one will talk to me. I'm hoping that Fiona will convince her aunt to cooperate with me."

"Who is Fiona?" Helen asked.

"My landlady at the moment. I thought I told you. She's the daughter of the doctor who delivered the triplets twenty-five years ago."

"Do you like her?" Helen asked.

"Maybe I do. I don't know. She's different from other women I've known."

"You mean she's different from Jill."

He didn't answer right away. When he did, he said, "You're right. She couldn't be more different."

"How old is she?"

He laughed. "Helen? What are you doing? What difference does it make?"

"I just wondered, that's all."

"Around twenty-five. She looks younger than that."

The Silhouette Reader Service™ — Here's how it works:

NO POSTAGE
NECESSARY
IF MAILED
IN THE
UNITED STATES

BUSINESS REPLY MAIL

FIRST-CLASS MAIL   PERMIT NO. 717-003   BUFFALO, NY

POSTAGE WILL BE PAID BY ADDRESSEE

SILHOUETTE READER SERVICE
3010 WALDEN AVE
PO BOX 1867
BUFFALO NY 14240-9952

Play the *Lucky Hearts* Game

and get...

2 FREE BOOKS
and a **FREE MYSTERY GIFT**...

Yes! **YOURS to KEEP!**

I have scratched off the silver card.
Please send me my *2 FREE BOOKS* and
FREE mystery GIFT. I understand that I am
under no obligation to purchase any books as
explained on the back of this card.

Scratch Here!

then look below to see
what your cards get you...
2 Free Books & a Free
Mystery Gift!

335 SDL DU6T   235 SDL DU7A

FIRST NAME   LAST NAME

ADDRESS

APT.#   CITY

STATE/PROV.   ZIP/POSTAL CODE   (S-SE-08/03)

Twenty-one gets you
2 FREE BOOKS
and a **FREE MYSTERY GIFT!**

Twenty gets you
2 FREE BOOKS!

Nineteen gets you
1 FREE BOOK!

TRY AGAIN!

Offer limited to one per household and not valid to current Silhouette Special Edition® subscribers. All orders subject to approval.

"I didn't realize you were staying in her home."

"Don't read anything into it, okay?"

Helen's chuckle sounded in his ear. "You're certainly becoming defensive, Greg. I wonder why?"

"Look, I've got to go. I'll give you a call tomorrow, okay?"

"Enjoy yourself," was Helen's parting shot.

Oh, great. Now he had his mother-in-law interested in his social life. She knew better than that. He had no social life.

He remembered the kiss from the night before. He'd felt weird being stirred up over a woman who was nothing like the women he'd dated before he married Jill.

It was the truth, what he'd said to Helen. He'd never met anyone like Fiona. Maybe that was why he found her so intriguing...so sexy...and so blasted hard to understand.

Last night she'd admitted that she was attracted to him. She'd come to him when he suggested the kiss. So what had changed overnight that she now treated him as if he were lower than dirt?

He poured his coffee and walked outside. McTavish bounded out with him and took off, no doubt chasing a rabbit. Greg sat on the bench in Fiona's garden and looked around. The Highlands were nothing like he'd imagined them. They were green, but there weren't many trees. From where he sat, he could see a herd of sheep moving down a hillside.

The area couldn't be more different from what he was used to in Queens. Then there was Fiona. Fiona, the rescuing angel who had taken him in and cared for him when he was too sick to care about anything. Fiona, the sprite, a magical creature who somehow managed to conceal her fragile wings from mere mortals.

He shook his head. Maybe it was the air around there that made him so whimsical. He didn't feel grounded in reality, which wasn't a good sign.

Greg finished his coffee and headed back to the house. He whistled for McTavish, who bounded toward him with comforting enthusiasm. At least he could rely on McTavish not to have unpredictable moods. Let's face it, he thought grimly, a dog was much easier to understand than a woman.

Fiona returned around noon and came in the back way, deliberately avoiding Greg. She slipped up the stairs without looking to see if he was in the living room or his bedroom.

Knowing that they would be traveling today, she had hurried through her visits. She'd alerted a neighbor to keep an eye on elderly Mrs. Grant, who was having some congestion. At her age, she could develop pneumonia with alarming ease.

Fiona found a small bag and quickly packed what she would need for an overnight stay in

Craigmor. She knew that her aunt would insist that she stay with her. She wasn't certain how Aunt Minnie would accept Greg. She lived in a rambling house with several bedrooms. If she were so inclined, Aunt Minnie could put them both up for the night with no problem.

Only time would tell.

She thought about calling her aunt to alert her she was coming to visit and that she was bringing someone with her, although she knew a phone call would be a waste of her time. Aunt Minnie had her housekeeper, Becky, answer the phone. She pretended to be too deaf to hear anything on the phone. Her strange malady disappeared as soon as she hung up. The truth, of course, was that Aunt Minnie disliked using a telephone to communicate. She thought it too impersonal.

Fiona gave herself a quick glance in the mirror and headed back downstairs. She dropped her bag at the foot of the stairs and walked into the living room.

McTavish dozed beside Greg's chair. Greg had a stack of files in front of him, methodically going through them. What a job he'd taken on.

McTavish raised his head and looked at her. Greg looked up, as well. "Oh. There you are. I didn't hear you come in."

"I thought I'd make sandwiches for lunch. When do you want to leave?"

He glanced at his watch. "I hadn't realized the

time. Probably as soon as we eat.'' He looked down at McTavish. ''What do you do with him when you travel?''

''He usually goes with me, but not this time. Patrick McKay from the village said he'd come pick him up and take him to his farm. McTavish enjoys visiting there.''

''And Tiger?''

''Tiger does not enjoy visiting, thank you very much. I leave extra food for him. He's found a way in and out of the house through the cellar. As long as he doesn't show his personal entrance to my home to any of his friends, I've allowed him to come and go as he pleases.'' She glanced around the room. ''He's probably outside now. I'll go make those sandwiches.''

Greg leaned back in his chair and absently scratched McTavish's head, surprised that the dog hadn't followed his mistress into the other room. *Maybe he's enjoying some male companionship,* he thought with an inward smile.

''So what do you think?'' he said in a low voice. ''Is she in a better mood? You know her better than I do. Do I need protection?''

McTavish pushed himself into a standing position with a groan and ambled out of the room. ''That bad, huh?'' Greg muttered.

At least she didn't waste time. They were in his car heading out within the hour. When Patrick Mc-Kay had arrived to pick up McTavish, the Scotsman had studied Greg with unconcealed curiosity. Greg had thought of several comments he might make, but had restrained himself. He'd heard about small towns and how everyone knew what everyone else was doing. Considering that Fiona lived alone, Greg thought this was a good thing.

He didn't like the idea of her living so far from neighbours. Granted, it was only a couple of miles to the road, but if she were to get hurt, it would be a very long two miles and, according to Patrick, it was another five miles into Glen Cairn.

Greg would probably have nightmares from now on about her living up here by herself, regardless of how protective McTavish was.

At least Greg didn't have to ask for directions to Craigmor. He had his marked map from the trip over there. After he glanced at it, he was ready to hit the road. Fiona sat quietly beside him and appeared to be miles away. She didn't have to make it any more obvious that she would prefer to be anywhere else than with him.

He'd gotten the message.

It was too bad for his peace of mind that she looked particularly fetching with her hair in a French braid. Jill had worn her hair that way occasionally before she cut it. On Jill the style was a sleek, smooth hairdo. On Fiona, wisps of soft curls fell around her ears and on the nape of her neck.

His fingers itched with the desire to run his fingers through her hair. He had to stop thoughts of that nature from distracting him. Yes, he was attracted to her. More, as a matter of fact, with every passing day. So what? He'd recover as soon as he left Scotland.

Wouldn't he?

"Tell me about your parents," he said into the silence.

"What about them?"

"Whatever you're willing to share."

Fiona settled back into her seat and smiled. Hopefully he'd chosen a safe enough topic to help her relax a little and enjoy the ride.

"My most vivid memories were how much they loved me. Aunt Minnie insists they spoiled me rotten. If I was spoiled, it was with their love, not material possessions. They were always so proud of me. They attended every social event I was in at school.

"I was a handful when I was young, or so Aunt Minnie assures me. Of course to have heard my parents tell it, I had no imperfections. Aunt Minnie made certain that I knew at a very early age not to believe that story! She said I led them on a merry chase and wore them out before each day ended."

"I'd love to see pictures of you when you were a child."

She looked at him in surprise. "You would? Why?"

"I don't know. Maybe to confirm my suspicions that you were a heartbreaker, even back then."

She didn't say anything and he wondered if he'd offended her. Again. When she finally spoke, she didn't reply to his comment. Instead, she said, "Aunt Minnie has pictures, if you'd like to see them."

"Yes," he said quietly. "I would." When she didn't say anything more, he asked, "Your aunt is your father's sister, isn't she?"

"Yes."

"I take it she never married, since she uses the name MacDonald."

"She was engaged. She grew up with Robbie, her fiancé. His dream was to learn to fly. He ended up in the RAF while she was finishing school. He was killed in a plane crash a few weeks before their wedding."

"That's tough. She must have loved him a great deal."

"Oh, I'm sure she did. By the time I was old enough to ask questions, though, she explained to me that Robbie was the only man brave enough to have considered marrying her."

He laughed. "I already like your aunt Minnie. I'm looking forward to meeting her."

"Just don't build too many expectations on the outcome of the meeting. She will be polite, I sincerely hope, but I really don't see her divulging much information. If she does, it will be a first."

Chapter Eight

The road followed the burn for several miles before reaching Craigmor. Fiona felt the familiar sadness that occurred each time she had returned to the village since her parents died. She wondered if she would ever stop expecting to find them at home waiting for her. She forced herself to look around, hoping to find something that had changed in the past two years.

Craigmor appeared to be the same. There was the greengrocer's shop, the meat market, the post office, and the church…all the places that had been part of her life when she lived there.

Greg's voice breaking into her reverie startled her. "Where do we go from here?" he asked.

"Oh! We turn by the church and follow the road that leads to the loch. I'll point out her home when we get there."

She made herself concentrate on the here and now. As much as she might wish to, she could change nothing in the past.

Greg followed the winding road until Fiona pointed to the driveway where they needed to turn.

The house couldn't be seen from the road because of the tall hedges Aunt Minnie had allowed to grow without trimming. They were now more bushy trees than shrubs, but her aunt preferred them that way.

When they pulled up in front of the house, Greg stopped the car and gazed at the stone structure. "Wow," he breathed. "This is close to a castle."

She smiled. "Close," she agreed. "It's several hundred years old. It's been in the MacDonald family for generations."

They left the car and walked up the broad, shallow stone steps to the wide double doors. Fiona took hold of the large ring hanging in the middle of one of the doors and banged it against the wood. She could hear the echo inside.

As usual, no one bothered to answer right away. Another one of Aunt Minnie's ploys. She always hoped that whoever came to the door would give up and go away.

After Fiona knocked for the third time, this time long and as loud as she could, she heard muttering on the other side of the door.

"I'm comin', I'm comin', so just hold your horses, would you?"

Fiona recognized the voice of Aunt Minnie's housekeeper/cook/general factotum. Aunt Minnie wouldn't survive a day without Miss Becky and she was the first one to admit it.

Becky opened the door, saw Fiona and rushed out to throw her arms around her. "Miss Fiona! Why in the world didn't you tell us you were comin', child? It's thrilled I am to see you. Miss Minnie will be beside herself!"

Fiona grinned. "I don't doubt that for a minute, Becky. However, she'll just have to deal with it, which is why I didn't call to warn her." She took a step back. "To add to my misdemeanors, I've brought someone to meet her."

Becky hadn't noticed Greg until Fiona gestured to where he stood, watching the meeting with his hands in his coat pockets. When she did, she placed her hand over her heart and said, "Don't tell me, Miss Fiona! Oh, Miss Minnie's going to have heart failure for sure." She spun on her heel and made a beeline back into the house, shouting, "Miss Minnie, Miss Minnie, you aren't going to believe it. Miss Fiona is here with her fella. Looks like we're finally going to have a wedding in this family. And it's about time, is what I say." Her voice gradually faded as she hurried down the hall-way. "And he's a real looker, too. Wait 'til you see him!"

Fiona had listened to the spate of words flowing out of Becky's mouth with first amusement, then astonishment and at the end, embarrassment. She turned and glanced at Greg who met her eyes with a steady gaze and a calm expression.

Maybe he hadn't heard Becky. Oh, please, God, please say he hadn't heard her. If she hadn't continued to stare at him, she would have missed the unholy gleam in his eye and the quick lift of the corner of his mouth that appeared and disappeared in a blink.

Her whole body flooded with color, completely wrapping around her to advertise her embarrassment. "I'm sorry, Greg," she began, only to have him interrupt her.

"There's nothing to apologize for. It was an honest mistake that we can quickly set straight."

She squared her shoulders. "You're right. Of course," she said, hoping to sound convincing. She turned and marched into the house without suggesting that he follow her. When the door closed behind her, she realized that he was indeed braving this next hurdle.

Of course he would follow her. Any sane person would have known that, but at the moment she was feeling anything but sane. She'd had some idea of rushing to Aunt Minnie and explaining the error before Greg reached her aunt. She gave her head a shake. That would have been rude in the extreme, which she wasn't. As a rule.

Fiona paused in the open doorway of her aunt's drawing room and saw her aunt move slowly toward the door. Aunt Minnie's arthritis must be acting up, which wouldn't improve her disposition any. Fiona had known this trip would be a disaster as soon as Greg mentioned it, but she'd had no idea it would become a farce, as well.

"Fiona!" Minnie said, advancing on her. Minnie was a tall woman, as slender as a reed, with a posture that would be the envy of any military man. She leaned down and gave Fiona a quick hug and a kiss on her cheek before her gaze narrowed on the man behind her.

"I don't believe we have met," she said to Greg in her most regal manner. She held out her hand in such a way as to make it difficult to know whether she expected him to shake it or kiss it. Fiona almost groaned aloud. He was already being tested before he'd had a chance to speak.

"Aunt Minnie," she rushed in to say, "I would like you to meet—"

"Let him speak for himself!" Minnie replied sharply, tapping her cane on the floor for emphasis.

Greg meanwhile took Minnie's hand and, with a grace that startled Fiona, delicately lifted her aunt's age-spotted hand and brushed his lips across her knuckles. "I'm Gregory Dumas, Miss Mac-

Donald,'' he said in a distinctively formal way. ''I am honored to meet you.''

Minnie jerked her hand away as though she'd been burned. ''You're an American! What is the world coming to?'' She spun on her heel and glared at Fiona. ''It was bad enough that you insisted on removing yourself to that desolate area but I will not tolerate the idea of you moving to America. Do you hear me?''

''Aunt Minnie,'' Fiona said, her heart racing until she wondered if she were on the verge of a stroke. ''You don't understand. I—''

''Of course I understand! I'm not an idiot nor am I some naive female who is easily appeased by falsehoods. I can certainly see how you might fall for the man. The way you keep yourself tucked out of sight, it's a wonder he ever found you at all. But a foreigner! How could you consider such a thing, Fiona?''

Greg exploded into laughter, a rich baritone that rolled off the walls of the room in waves. Fiona stared at him in astonishment. So did Minnie.

He started to speak, then looked at the two women staring at him with their jaws dropped and continued to laugh. It was obvious he was attempting to control himself. He would pause and start to speak only to start laughing again.

Minnie turned to Fiona. ''What *is* the matter with the man? Is he daft?''

Fiona lifted her shoulders and spread her hands,

which, for some reason, encouraged Greg's laughter.

"I'm so sorry," he finally managed to say, gasping. He pulled a handkerchief from his back pocket and mopped his face and eyes. "I didn't mean to be rude. It's just that—" he paused to swallow a chuckle "—I feel as though I walked into the middle of a farce with no idea what my lines are supposed to be."

Strange that he would also see the farcical qualities of the meeting, Fiona thought. She wondered if Greg had any idea how attractive he was when he laughed.

She smiled at him. "Actually, I was thinking the same thing." She shared a grin with Greg.

"I do wish you would tell me what's going on here," Minnie said in a voice that could have just as easily said, "Off with his head!"

Before Fiona could speak, Becky appeared in the doorway behind them and said. "Dinner is served," as though addressing royalty.

Fiona saw Greg clench his jaw and stare fixedly at the ceiling, refusing to meet her eyes.

Minnie turned back to Fiona. "Well, then, come along. You can explain how you met and when you're planning to marry your young man over dinner." She turned to Greg with a stern expression. "I shall warn you right now, Mr. Dumas, you will not, under any circumstances, take Fiona away with you. This is her home and I mean for her to spend her life here.''

Greg immediately dropped his gaze to his booted feet and nodded as solemnly as possible, considering he looked as though he was biting the inside of his cheek.

''Aunt Minnie—'' Fiona began in a strangled voice.

Minnie held up her hand. ''Not now, dear. We shall discuss everything over dinner.'' She looked at Greg. ''You may escort me to dinner, young man.''

Greg surprised Fiona by immediately holding out his arm so that Minnie could take it. Leaning slightly on him and with head high, Minnie proceeded with dignity into the formal dining room— the one that held a table where forty could be easily seated. Several of the leaves had been removed, Fiona was thankful to see, and Becky had set the three places at one end of the table…with Minnie at the end and Greg and Fiona facing each other.

Fiona refused to meet his gaze.

After Greg seated Minnie, she asked him to say grace.

Another test, Fiona thought, wanting to scream at her aunt. Instead, she bowed her head and made a silent prayer of her own, although she doubted that God would grant her prayer to whisk her back to the sanity of her own home to the time before Greg Dumas came into her life.

Then Greg spoke. He sounded as though the ritual of grace was familiar to him. He was brief but eloquent and when he finished Fiona couldn't help but notice Minnie's smug smile.

So far it appeared that Greg had passed Aunt Minnie's impromptu tests but Fiona didn't hold out much hope that he could keep up with her aunt for the entire evening. She began to mull over where they might spend the night if they left here immediately after dinner.

The food was delicious and she told Becky so when Becky retrieved their plates and brought them dessert. There was no hint that Becky had been anything other than prepared to have visitors. Fiona wondered how she had managed.

"Now then, young man," Minnie said over dessert, "tell me how you and Fiona met."

Fiona quickly said, "Aunt Minnie, I'm afraid you don't under—"

"Nonsense! I understand perfectly well. He took one look at you and fell in love, which is a mark in his favor. He knows quality when he sees it. Now, then, let him speak, Fiona. You and I can visit later."

Fiona dropped her head into her hand and closed her eyes.

Greg spoke, his voice sounding suspiciously amused. At least he didn't break into another fit of laughter. Fiona wished that she could find the situation amusing instead of its being the most embarrassing situation she'd ever experienced.

"I came to Scotland in search of birth records for my client, who recently discovered she was adopted in Edinburgh, Scotland, twenty-five years ago. My search led me to Fiona," he said.

"How could Fiona possibly help you?" Minnie asked impatiently.

"I was told that Dr. MacDonald might have additional information regarding the adoption. When I discovered he had died, I looked up his daughter in the hope she had the files that might give more details on the adoption.

"I turned up at Fiona's home several nights ago, lost and running a fever. She took me in, dosed me with some mysterious and potent hot drinks and when I was better she gave me permission to look through her father's files."

Minnie turned to Fiona. "Why would you allow such a thing?"

Becky appeared in the doorway as though waiting to hear the answer, as well. Fiona wondered how long Becky had been loitering just out of sight.

"I saw no reason to deny him access." She met her aunt's steely gaze without blinking.

"Those files are private, Fiona. They should have been destroyed when your father died."

"Perhaps. But they weren't, so I let Greg look at them while he was recovering from his illness."

"He has been staying in your home?" she asked incredulously, as though that piece of information had only now registered.

"He wasn't well, Aunt Minnie. I decided to care for him there."

Minnie turned to Greg. "You seduced her, didn't you?" she asked with unfeigned disgust. "You horrid man. While you had the files as an excuse to be there, you had the perfect opportunity to seduce my niece!"

"Aunt Minnie! How can you say that? He has been a gentleman throughout the time he's been here!"

There was no humor in Greg's face when he replied. "No, Miss MacDonald, I did not seduce your niece. Regardless of what you think, I am an honorable man. I do not take advantage of people, male or female. I certainly don't prey on innocent women. Your unfounded accusation is insulting not only to me but to your niece, as well." He pushed his chair away from the table. "If you'll excuse me." He stood and left the room. The two women sat there, listening to his footsteps echoing on the tiled floor of the foyer, then the front door opening and quietly closing.

Silence echoed around them.

Minnie finally spoke, her voice subdued. "Where do you suppose he's going?

Fiona studied her hands in her lap. She didn't look up at the question. She shook her head.

Becky walked silently into the room carrying a coffee tray. When Minnie saw her, she said, "Thank you, dear. I believe we'll have coffee in the library. There's a fire there, isn't there?"

"Yes, ma'am."

Minnie stood and looked around her as though uncertain what to do next. She glanced at Fiona who had also risen. "I offended him."

"Yes."

"One of the curses of growing old, I'm afraid. My thoughts suddenly leap out of my mouth before I can stop them. I didn't mean to offend him."

Fiona offered her arm to her aunt who gratefully took it. They walked out of the room and followed Becky into the library.

Once they were seated, Fiona asked, "What did you mean to do? You've been interrogating him since we walked through the door, as though he planned to steal all the silver in the house. I've never seen you this rude before, Aunt Minnie. Abrupt and impatient, perhaps. But never rude."

Minnie made a face. "I know. My behavior was inexcusable. I wanted to protect you, I suppose. I wasn't thinking about how my words sounded." She held her saucer with one hand and sipped her coffee with the other. "He's a very nice young man, you know. I can see why you're in love with him."

"It isn't like that, Aunt Minnie. I've been at-tempting to tell you since we arrived that he isn't my young man as Becky thought. He's here on business, that's all. I provided him a place to stay. He's returning home soon, with or without the information he came to find. I thought you might be able to help him. I had no idea there would be such a huge misunderstanding at the time we arrived, or I might not have brought him to see you. There is no romantic relationship. I want to make that very clear.''

Minnie carefully set her cup on the saucer and, equally carefully, placed the saucer on the table next to her chair.

''There's no reason to lie to me, dear. I understand what it's like to love a man.''

''Aunt Minnie! You aren't listening to me. I am not romantically involved with Greg Dumas!''

Minnie studied her face for several moments before she said, ''I see. Yes,'' she continued, nodding her head, ''I see that now.''

''What are you talking about?'' Fiona asked, feeling more and more exasperated.

''You aren't aware you're in love with him. That's not surprising, really. You've never been one to spend much time with young men. I always suspected that when you finally fell, you would fall hard.''

Fiona wondered if her aunt had slipped away into senile dementia without anyone noticing. Perhaps she would have noticed if she had visited

Craigmor more often, she thought with a sense of guilt.

She reached for her aunt's hand. "You're tired, Aunt Minnie," she said softly. "We've kept you up too late. Perhaps tomorrow you'll be feeling more yourself."

Minnie drew herself up. "Young woman, there is no reason to speak to me as though I'm dotty just because you haven't recognized your own malady. On the other hand, if you have, you've conveniently put it out of your mind. Would it help you to know that he's very much attracted to you, as well?"

"No, he isn't. From the little I've been able to discover about him, he lost his wife. He's still grieving—that much I do know."

"Perhaps he was, when he arrived in Scotland. However, you have shaken him, made him aware that he's still alive. He probably doesn't like that very much," she added with an understanding nod.

Fiona doggedly pointed out, "He has a young daughter. I'm not sure how old she is."

"So if things work out between the two of you, you would be starting your married life with a ready-made family."

Fiona jumped up from her chair, wanting to pull her hair. She paced across the room and stared unseeingly at a row of books. "Why can't I get you to understand that we are not in love with each other and we have no intention of getting married?

The idea is ludicrous,'' she said, working not to raise her voice.

Her aunt sounded amused. ''I understand your frustration, Fiona. I'm having the same problem with getting you to understand that you're refusing to face what's going on between the two of you. Why, the electricity between you is so strong it could light up the entire house. Deny it if you will.''

Fiona spun around. Her aunt calmly watched her, looking unruffled and very sane. Fiona's heart began to pound erratically and she had trouble breathing. Minnie nodded wisely.

''Becky knew as soon as she saw you with him. You haven't tried to hide it, you know. You glow with your love for him. It shows every time you look at him, every time he speaks. Surely you had some inkling...'' She paused, looking at Fiona in dismay. ''I'm sorry you find the knowledge so painful, my dear.''

Fiona had returned to her chair and sat while her aunt spoke. By the time Minnie finished speaking, tears ran down Fiona's face.

''I didn't know,'' she whispered.

''Or you didn't want to know.''

''He's going back to New York. He may have left tonight for all I know.''

Minnie shook her head. ''No, dear. He'll be back. He left rather than be rude to an old woman who was prying into matters that don't concern her. He won't abandon you here. Believe me. He'll return once he's gained some control.'' She leaned forward. ''If I'd had any doubts about his feelings where you are concerned, they were dispersed when he came so vehemently to your defense.'' She touched Fiona's hand in a soothing gesture. ''The two of you have chosen a difficult path, but I'm a firm believer in the tenet that love will find a way.''

She poured Fiona another cup. ''Have some more coffee and then go on up to bed. I'll wait down here for Mr. Dumas. I owe him an apology. I won't be able to sleep until it's delivered.''

''Why are you so sure he'll come back?''

Minnie smiled. ''Where else would he go? You say he came to speak with me, didn't you? In addition, he needs to return you to your home. Sooner or later, he'll be back. I'm wagering that it will be sooner.''

''If you're wrong?''

''It won't be the first time I've slept in this chair in front of a nice, warm fire. Probably won't be the last.''

Fiona didn't know what to do. She was exhausted from the emotional strain of the past several hours…from the past several days, for that matter. She set her cup on the table and said, ''Then I'll go on up. Where do you want me to sleep?''

''In your old bedroom, of course. We'll talk more in the morning.''

Minnie watched her niece leave the room, her heart aching for the young girl. Whoever said that love was a wonderful state to be in was an idiot. Being in love was painful, particularly when it might be one-sided.

Each of these two young people was at that stage in their relationship. The situation would be almost comical if it weren't so serious. Minnie had never considered that someday Fiona might move away from Scotland. Fiona was her only relative…her only heir. When she died, Fiona would inherit this home and its contents. In addition she'd already received a well-endowed trust fund from her parents that would continue to provide all her needs for the rest of her life.

Minnie leaned her head against the chair and closed her eyes. ''Ah, Robbie. If only you were here to guide me through this. You were always wise beyond your years…and so sensible about things. Will there ever come a time in my life when I won't wake up missing you, or fall asleep yearning for you?''

She dozed until the sound of a car in the driveway brought her to full wakefulness some time later. She pushed her way out of the chair and started for the front door, doing her best to hurry before he knocked. There was no reason to disturb the other two occupants of the house at this hour.

Becky needed her sleep and Fiona had worried herself into exhaustion.

Minnie opened the door just as Greg reached the top step. He paused on the edge of the landing and looked at her.

"I owe you an apology, Mr. Dumas," Minnie said briskly. "Please come inside so that I don't have to contract frostbite to deliver it."

She wasn't sure he was going to comply. When he did, he made his reluctance plain.

"I came to get Fiona," he said, slowly walking toward her.

"Yes, I know. I sent her to bed some time ago. Please come inside."

She stepped back and allowed him to move past her. She smelled the distinctive odor of ale and nodded to herself. The pub had been an understandable choice for him to make. Perhaps a drink or two had eased his anger somewhat.

Minnie led the way into the library. Becky had built up the fire before she went to bed but it was now down to embers. Without asking, Greg knelt in front of the fire and replenished its supply of fuel.

"There's some coffee left. I'm afraid it's cold by now."

"Doesn't matter," he said, rising from the hearth.

She sat in her chair and motioned for him to sit in the one that Fiona had occupied earlier.

"I don't usually blurt out everything that pops into my mind like I did tonight. I'm afraid I was inexcusably rude and for that I am sorry. Becky has made up a bed for you. It's upstairs and to the left. The second door on the right. I believe you'll find it comfortable."

Greg leaned forward and placed his elbows on his knees, his clasped hands between them. "I'm afraid you've accepted me into your home under false pretences, Miss MacDonald. Fiona and I are not a couple. We are not planning a wedding. I'm here on business. That's all."

She nodded. "I know. Fiona explained all of that after you left."

"I know it was rude of me to leave that way. I just—" He stopped, obviously searching for words.

"You didn't want to strangle a doddering old fool and decided a timely retreat was in order." She smiled. "Yes, I know."

He looked startled, then nodded. "Something like that," he admitted ruefully.

She settled back into her chair. "Tell me, young man. How can I assist you in your search?"

"By telling me the last name of a couple whose first names were Moira and Douglas. Moira gave birth in the fall of 1978 and your brother delivered her three daughters. What I need to find out is Moira's last name."

"I'm afraid I can't help you. They must not

have been from Craigmor because I've never heard of them.''

He rubbed his face and sighed. The only sound in the room was the quiet snapping of the fire.

''I'm curious,'' Minnie asked a little later. ''What do you intend to do if you're unable to find the information you seek?''

He shrugged. ''Go home. There's nothing else I can do.''

''I wish I had the information you're seeking.''

''So do I. I would have thought the birth of triplets would have caused quite a stir in the village.''

''Yes, you mentioned daughters, didn't you? Triplets, is it? I would certainly have heard if someone had given birth to triplets.''

''That was what I was counting on. However, I've searched through boxes of files and found nothing. I'm beginning to believe there's nothing to be found.'' He rubbed his temple as though he had a headache.

Minnie watched him for a while as he stared into the fire. When she spoke, he looked startled, either by her voice or her subject matter.

''Fiona tells me you have a daughter. How old is she?''

He blinked, his mind obviously on other matters. Fiona knew that he had a daughter? ''My daughter?'' he repeated, suddenly remembering that he'd been talking to Tina one afternoon when Fiona came home. ''She's five.''

"Five. A lovely age. So inquisitive, so full of life."

"She is that, all right."

"Before you retire for the night, I was wondering if you'd like to see some of Fiona's childhood pictures."

His eyes narrowed. Had Fiona mentioned to her aunt that he wanted to see childhood pictures of her? He'd like to tell her to forget it, but the truth was, he was curious about Fiona. Besides, there was nothing wrong with looking at photographs, if that would make her aunt happy. "I suppose so," he said slowly.

"Do you see those photo albums on the third shelf over there?" she asked, nodding to one of the walls filled with books. "Would you mind bringing them to me? There are three albums."

Greg crossed the room, slid the albums from the shelf and returned to the area where Minnie sat watching him. "I believe they're self-explanatory. If you have any questions, I'll do my best to answer them."

Greg opened the first album. He felt guilty at looking through them without Fiona's knowledge or permission and yet his curiosity impelled him. Greg leafed through the albums and followed the pictorial chronicle of Fiona's life, carefully recorded by an untold amount of snapshots.... And Jill had accused *him* of being a shutterbug.

He continued to turn the pages and watched as

the bright-eyed sprite of a baby became a toddler, a little girl, a gangly child and a petite teenager. Many of the photos were with an older couple.

"I take it these are her parents," he said.

Minnie smiled. "The photographs are of my brother, James, and his wife. Fiona was adopted."

"Yes, she told me that in reality she's their niece."

"So Fiona thinks."

"What do you mean?".

"I have no idea why, but Jamie and Meggie chose to tell her they were related to her."

"They weren't?"

"Meggie was an only child and I'm Jamie's only sibling."

"Fiona has never suspected?"

"No. However, I am curious. You discovered that your client was one of triplets. What is your client's birthdate?"

He'd already checked his notes since discussing it with Fiona. "November 28, 1978."

"Interesting. Fiona's birthday is November 28 of the same year."

"Yes, she told me she'd been born in the fall of that year. I—" He stopped speaking and stared at Minnie. "You don't suppose—?"

"I have no way of knowing, of course, but I suspect Fiona and your client may be part of the set. I must admit you gave me quite a start when you mentioned triplets. I never knew about there being multiple births.''

He hesitated, then asked, ''You knew I was here in Craigmor before, didn't you?''

She nodded. ''Of course. I had no reason to think I could give you any information regarding triplets.''

''Why did you choose to tell me about Fiona, since she doesn't know?''

''I hesitate to answer that question. I've said a great deal tonight, some of which I sincerely regret. I don't want to regret anything more.''

''I won't be so quick to take offense next time,'' he said softly.

''I have no way of knowing who Fiona's parents were. If she is one of the triplets, I believe she should be told. Although I don't want her to think badly about the story Jamie and Meggie told her, I also don't want to deprive her of the possibility of meeting members of her family.''

''So you told me because—?''

She chose her words carefully. ''I told you because I realized this evening that Fiona might have formed an attachment of sorts toward you. If that is the case, I feel it imperative that I tell you the little I know about the circumstances surrounding her birth. Your investigation may have a strong impact on Fiona. I want to make certain you understand all the ramifications.''

''You're not suggesting that I tell her, are you?''

''Not until and unless you find proof. I see no reason to tell her, otherwise. Knowing my brother, I seriously doubt he left anything in writing since he went to so much trouble to create such an elaborate deception.''

''So you're saying I won't find anything. I tend to agree with you. If there was anything to be found, I believe I would have discovered it by now.'' He sighed. ''I need to return to New York and tell my client what I found.''

''Which is the truth. By the way, how old are you, Mr. Dumas?''

''Thirty-three.''

''Ah.''

He looked at her suspiciously. ''What does that mean?''

She chuckled. ''I'm not being inscrutable, Mr. Dumas. Just curious.''

Greg leaned back in the chair and stared at the fire. He'd never been one to admit defeat, but he knew the trail he'd been following had dried up. There was no sense in fooling himself. It was time for him to return to his regular routine and the responsibilities that awaited him at home.

He hoped Fiona's aunt was wrong. He didn't want Fiona emotionally attached to him. Despite his strong physical attraction to her, he knew he would end up hurting her.

Jill was the first person he'd loved and he learned that love made him vulnerable. He found it easier to revert to the lessons he'd learned as a child—if he didn't get close to anyone, he couldn't get hurt.

Fiona deserved much more than he could offer her.

Chapter Nine

Fiona entered the dining room the following morning and found Greg eating a hearty breakfast. He sat back in his chair when he saw her and smiled. "Good morning," he said.

Becky came in from the kitchen. "I have your breakfast warming, Miss Fiona," she said. "Miss Minnie isn't coming down this morning. She asked me to bring her breakfast on a tray."

"Is she ill?" Fiona asked, concerned.

"No, ma'am. She's just tired."

"I'm afraid that's my fault," Greg said quietly when Becky returned to the kitchen for Fiona's breakfast. "We sat and talked for a long while last night. I shouldn't have kept her up so late."

Fiona slipped into the chair she'd occupied for dinner and stared at Greg. He looked rested and at ease. "The late hours seemed to have agreed with you," she finally said.

"Not so much the late hours, but the realization that I've gone as far as I can on this case and it's time to admit defeat. There's a certain amount of relief in admitting it to myself." He smiled ruefully. "That and a couple of beers I had at a local pub. Helped me to relax."

"I wasn't sure that you'd come back, but there was never a doubt in Aunt Minnie's mind."

"She's quite a woman, your aunt. I'm impressed with her."

"You are? After what she said to you?"

"Actually, she was incensed on your behalf. She didn't know me, so she was suspicious of my motives. By the time I finished the second beer I realized that her reaction was understandable given the circumstances. I shouldn't have been so quick to take offense, but I'll admit I was pretty steamed when I left last night."

Becky set Fiona's plate in front of her as well as a porcelain teapot, refilled Greg's cup with more coffee and left the room.

"I take it she wasn't able to help you, if you're giving up your search."

Fiona poured herself some tea.

"She'd never heard of Moira and Douglas, which leads me to conclude they weren't from this area. I had begun to suspect that. Although she was intrigued by the thought of triplets, she couldn't recall hearing anything about them. So that's where I am. I don't believe that anyone alive has more than the information I already have."

"How sad."

"Yes, it is."

She forced herself to smile. "So you'll be returning to the States."

"Yes. If you don't mind, we'll leave for Glen Cairn after breakfast. I need to call the airlines and book my return flight now and then go back to your place and grab my bag."

"Of course." Fiona couldn't force herself to say anything more. They ate in silence. When she finished, she excused herself and went upstairs to check on her aunt.

She paused in front of Minnie's door and gently tapped.

"Come in, Fiona," Minnie called. "You don't need to stand on ceremony."

Fiona opened the door and walked inside. Minnie was propped up in bed by a plethora of pillows, daintily sipping from a cup.

"Are you feeling all right?" Fiona asked, crossing the room to Minnie's side. She touched her fingers to her aunt's forehead and was relieved to find that she felt cool. At least she had no fever.

In the morning light, Aunt Minnie showed each one of her eighty years. Fine lines feathered across her face. Her eyes were as clear as ever, her gaze sharp. Fiona realized how much she loved her aunt, despite—or perhaps because of—her many eccentricities.

"We're leaving now, Aunt Min. I've enjoyed seeing you again."

"You don't visit enough. You know that as well as I do. I understood your reasons for leaving. I miss Jamie and Meggie, too, but you've had time to deal with their deaths. I think it's time you moved in with me, don't you?"

Fiona sank into the chair beside the bed. "There *is* something wrong, isn't there? Have you been to the doctor? What did he say? Did he run tests?" Try as she might, Fiona was unable to use her ability to see colors or pick up anything on her aunt. Perhaps it was because she was emotionally involved with her. Then again, her aunt had always been difficult to read, regardless of her physical health.

"Fiona, dear. There is nothing wrong with me other than the fact that I've used this body for a long, long while. I tire more easily these days. Therefore, I rest more. That's sensible, not an illness. I refuse to play the pity card in hope that you will come back to watch over me. I want you to come because this is your home and we're family.

There. I did play the pity card, after all. Of course you can see right through it.''

Fiona laughed, as Aunt Minnie wanted.

''What are your young man's plans this morning, besides taking you home?''

''Aunt Minnie, he is *not*—''

''Just a figure of speech, dear. There's no reason for you to become hostile.''

''He's downstairs booking his return flight to New York. He'll be leaving as soon as possible.''

''Too bad. I like him.''

''Well, the two of you have certainly formed a mutual admiration society.''

Aunt Minnie looked pleased. ''That's reassuring, I must say. Please have him come tell me goodbye, would you, dear?''

Fiona wanted to roll her eyes. But she didn't. ''Yes, ma'am.'' She leaned over and kissed her aunt's cheek. ''I love you, Aunt Min.''

Minnie patted Fiona's face. ''I feel the same way about you. You've been such a blessing to all of our lives, dear.''

Fiona smiled. ''I'm glad.'' She straightened and stroked Minnie's hair. ''I'll send Greg up.''

Minnie watched Fiona move across the room with her graceful, gliding step. She had truly been a blessing to each member of the family.

Minnie knew she'd taken a calculated risk telling Greg about the mystery surrounding Fiona's birth. He needed to know. There was the strong possibility that his client was one of Fiona's sisters. If that was true, Fiona should know that she had other family besides an aging, crotchety aunt.

This was going to be an interesting time in Fiona's life. Her one regret was that Jamie and Meggie weren't here to explain things. There was so much she didn't know and it surprised her that her brother hadn't taken her into his confidence. If he had, she might be better able to help today.

Fiona had left the bedroom door open. Greg paused in the doorway and tapped lightly on the doorjamb. "You're looking quite chipper this morning, considering what little sleep you had," he said, walking to the side of the bed without hesitation. He took Minnie's hand between his.

Minnie chuckled. "I can't tell you how relieved I am to hear you say that. The way Fiona acted just now, you'd think I was fading fast, not expected to last through the day."

Greg laughed. "You're a marvel. You know that, don't you?"

"Well, of course I do," she replied with raised brows. "I presumed you noticed that about me first thing."

"As a matter of fact…" he said, allowing his words to trail off. "Seriously, meeting you has been worth all the wasted days of chasing my tail looking for information."

"Really. So meeting Fiona is incidental, I take it?"

His smile faded. "I worry about her."

"Yes. So do I."

"She's too isolated where she is now," he said quietly.

Minnie nodded. "We were discussing that very thing a few minutes ago." She paused. "What about you?" she asked.

He looked puzzled. "I'm afraid I don't follow."

"Have you ever considered moving to Scotland?"

His laugh was rueful. "No, Miss Minnie, I have never considered the idea. I'm a native New Yorker. Besides, my daughter, Tina, would be devastated if I were to take her away from her grandparents. They've added stability to both our lives."

"Ah. Perhaps you should suggest they visit here. They might be willing to relocate, as well."

Greg found the whole idea absurd. "I take it you're with the local chamber of commerce?"

Minnie nodded, returning to her regal mode, he thought, amused. "You could at least consider my idea."

"Of course." Consider and dismiss, but he didn't need to say that to her. "Thank you for your hospitality, Miss MacDonald. It has certainly been an enlightening visit, all things considered."

"Yes, it has. By the way, were you able to book your flight?"

"Oh. Yes. I'll need to get back to Glasgow tomorrow evening in order to catch the flight first thing the next morning.''

''I see. Well, then, you need to be off, I'm sure.''

He leaned over and placed a light kiss on Minnie's forehead. ''Take care of yourself.''

She closed her eyes and smiled. ''You may count on it,'' she said, opening them when he drew away from her. ''I intend to be around for a long while.''

Greg left the room bemused. He felt as though there had been two levels to the conversation going on back there.

Where had Fiona's aunt come up with the idea that he'd consider moving to Scotland? As soon as he had the thought, he knew the answer. Fiona. She wanted him to move to Scotland because of Fiona.

So she was playing matchmaker, was she? Well, it was too bad that she considered him a mate for her niece. She was in for nothing but disappointment if that was the case.

He had no intention of getting involved with anyone again. He had Tina. That was enough family. George and Helen provided her with grandparents. There was no reason to upset the family dynamics by bringing another person into the mix.

It was at that point in his musings that he realized Fiona was watching him descend the stairs from where she stood near the front door, her bag at her feet.

A golden glow flooded the area from the window on the landing of the stairwell, framing her in light. When he made eye contact with her, she smiled, looking very young and vulnerable, her hair glowing like a nimbus around her.

His chest ached with unnamed emotions.

He paused when he reached her side and picked up his overnight bag, which he'd left beside the door. Without saying anything, he took hers from her and walked toward the door. Fiona opened it and he strode through and down the steps to the car.

She closed the door behind them and followed him.

Once they were on the road again, she said, "You looked grim when you left Aunt Minnie. Did she give you trouble?" Her voice held a hint of surprise.

"No. I've got a lot on my mind right now."

"Oh. Did you book your flight?"

"Yeah. I need to be in Glasgow by tomorrow evening."

When she said nothing more he gave her a quick glance. He enjoyed looking at her profile. Now that he was looking for it, he could see a family resemblance between his client and Fiona, although their eyes and hair were not the same color. The triplets must have been fraternal.

Both women were small in stature with delicate

features. Each of them was beautiful but he'd never had the reaction to his client that he had to Fiona.

He groaned and she immediately asked, "What's wrong? Are you in pain?"

"I'm all right. I guess you'll be glad to get me out of your hair and return to your regular life."

"It will be an adjustment, but I'll manage," she replied.

"Yeah, I thought you would."

He would adjust, as well. He tried to convince himself that his strong attraction to her was the result of their having spent so much time together these past several days. Plus he hadn't been with a woman since Jill died. Hadn't wanted to be, as far as that goes. His response to her beauty meant he was a normal, functioning male.

Once he left, he'd quickly recover from whatever fever she stirred in his blood.

They reached Glen Cairn midafternoon. Instead of turning into her lane, Greg continued through the village with Fiona giving him directions until they reached Patrick McKay's farm. As soon as they pulled up, McTavish came bounding toward the car, barking with delight.

They stepped out of the car—Fiona to let Patrick's wife know she was taking McTavish home and Greg to open the back seat car door. McTavish raced around Fiona with enthusiasm, then dashed over to where Greg stood. McTavish greeted him with equal exuberance. By the time Fiona returned to the car, McTavish was in the back seat, looking like royalty ready to greet and wave to his loyal subjects.

Fiona was laughing at McTavish's antics. "You'd think I'd been away for weeks and weeks from the way he's acting."

"It's nice to be greeted with so much energy and yet so much restraint. Any other dog would have been jumping on us, but not McTavish."

Fiona slid into the car and looked at McTavish. "Of course not. You are a well-behaved young man, are you not?"

McTavish whuffled in agreement, causing Greg to smile. "He understands you, doesn't he?"

"Absolutely, unless he becomes selectively deaf. That generally happens when he's chasing a rabbit and I call him to come inside."

"Can't blame him there."

With McTavish as a buffer, the mood lightened considerably by the time they reached Fiona's home. As soon as Greg released McTavish, he took off to check out any new smells that had been left around the property while he was away. Tiger sauntered out from wherever he'd been, stretched, yawned and blinked at them.

"Quite a greeting all the way around," Greg said. He grabbed their bags and followed her in through her front entrance.

The house was chilled. He set his bag inside his room, placed hers at the bottom of the stairs and went into the living room to build a fire. As soon as that was accomplished, Greg went into his room and closed the door.

The combination of lack of sleep the night before and the strong emotions he'd been battling most of the day had taken their toll. He stretched out on the bed and was asleep within minutes.

Fiona went into the kitchen and began preparations for supper. She'd been quiet most of the way home, thinking about what her life would be like once Greg left.

The fact that she'd dreamed about him most of the previous night hadn't helped. In one of her dreams, she had run after him when he'd left, begging him to stay with her, crying when he told he had to go home.

Another dream had him returning to the house late at night, coming up the stairs to her room and lying down beside her. He'd awakened her with his kisses, stirring her to respond and to help him remove his clothes. She had kissed and caressed him, reveling in the opportunity to make love to him. She'd awakened suddenly from that dream, her skin tingling as though he had been touching her in the same way. She would never admit to anyone but herself that she had been disappointed to find it had only been a dream.

She fed her animals, set the table and ladled up the food into serving dishes before she went to find

Greg. She hadn't heard a word from him since they'd arrived home.

The living room was empty, although the fire had taken the chill off the room. He'd built a fire, it seemed. He was a little too good at that particular skill, and she wasn't necessarily referring to the one in the fireplace.

She went to the door of his room and tapped. There was no answer. She opened the door to make certain he wasn't there before she went searching for him outside. When she saw him asleep on the bed she knew she wouldn't need to search any further.

He lay on his stomach, his arms flung out on either side. His feet, still in boots, hung over the edge. He must have been exhausted not to remove them.

"Greg?" she said. "Dinner is ready."

There was no answer.

She walked over to the bed. "Greg."

No response.

Fiona sat on the side of the bed and gently rubbed his back. She could feel the heat of his body through his sweater, pick up the slight scent of his aftershave, which could have been invented especially for him. Without giving the action much thought, she slipped her hand beneath the sweater and T-shirt he wore, luxuriating in the feel of his bare, muscular back, the indentation of his spine and the beginning of a curve where the waist of his jeans blocked her from moving farther.

He shifted, slowly rolling away from her onto his back. He yawned and opened his eyes. "That was nice," he murmured.

"What was?"

"Waking up to a back rub."

"I apologize for being so personal," she said, knowing her face was a fiery red. She forced herself to meet his gaze. "I kept sponging you off while you were sick in an effort to bring down your fever. I suppose I grew used to touching you…." Her voice trailed off.

"Fiona…" His eyes darkened.

"I know. There's nothing between us. There can be nothing between us. It's just that…" Her voice trailed off.

He reached up and brushed the back of his hand across her cheek. "I don't ever want to hurt you," he said. "Or take advantage of you in any way."

Fiona knew that if she let Greg walk out of her life without having experienced his lovemaking, she would regret it for the rest of her life. She wanted no regrets. Not where Greg was concerned.

With a calm deliberation, Fiona stood and briskly peeled off her clothes down to her bra and panties. Greg, startled, sat up and said, "What are you doing?"

Of course he knew what she was doing, she thought, as she sat beside him once more. His gaze seemed to sweep over her in waves and everywhere his gaze paused, she tingled.

"I'm seducing you," she said, sounding breathless, as she slid her arms around his neck and kissed him.

Chapter Ten

Fiona gave a fleeting thought to the meal waiting for them in the kitchen. She couldn't believe she had been so brazen as to suggest that—

Well, that she would be willing to—

That she would even consider the possibility of—

She shifted so that she could draw closer to him. He was breathing hard, but then, so was she. She wanted—quite desperately, in fact—to make love with Greg, and now that she had so baldly stated her desire, she was afraid he would reject her.

He hadn't moved since she'd placed her arms

around him and yet his lips were soft and so very kissable that she decided he didn't mind.

When his arms came around her in a fierce grip and he began to kiss her back, she almost laughed with relief. It was going to be all right. Everything would be all right.

After several mind-blowing minutes, Greg pulled away from her. "I don't think this is a very good idea," he began, and she placed her fingers against his mouth.

"Don't think. Don't analyze. Just be here with me right here…and right now. I'm asking nothing of you, Greg. I want no promises or insincere words." She tugged on his sweater until he lifted his arms and she pulled it over his head. The T-shirt disappeared the same way.

When she reached for his belt buckle, she found his hand there, already unfastening the belt and pants. Within moments his boots were off with his pants and he was bare.

Oh, my, but he had an exquisite body. She rested her hand on his taut belly, her eyes widening when he shivered. She started to pull away when he trapped her hand beneath his, holding her there, inches away from a very long erection. How was it possible to— No. She didn't want to go there, even in her thoughts.

"Don't be afraid to touch me," he murmured. "I promise not to bite." His smile wavered when she followed his instructions. "Although…I might nibble a little, if you say it's all right."

She knew that she was being outrageous and she didn't care. He would be leaving soon and she would never see him again. She wanted this time with him and although he had protested, he had not pushed her away.

No, he had not pushed her away.

Instead, he had lowered himself back onto the bed and watched her, waiting to see what she would do next. She wondered the same thing.

She felt hot, then cold. She closed her eyes and focused on the warmth of his skin beneath her palm. He dropped his hand to his side.

Greg's muscles were hard and his skin was smooth. With no resistance on his part, she skimmed her hand up his chest and circled the tiny, tightly beaded nipples almost buried in nests of silky hair.

He quivered and closed his eyes, smiling as he gave himself up to her ministrations.

Fiona forgot about the meal cooling in the other room. All she remembered were the feelings he evoked deep inside of her, feelings so intense she could scarcely contain them.

She wanted this man. She needed to be fiercely honest with herself about that. Tonight would be the last time she would see him. Was she going to let this opportunity slip away without taking advantage of these last few hours with him?

Fiona shivered, feeling the slight chill of the room ripple across her bare skin. When she glanced at his face, she realized that Greg was watching her, his eyes dark with an expression that she could readily identify.

Feeling more than a little awkward, Fiona stretched out on her side beside him, leaning her head against her hand while she rested on her elbow.

"You are more exquisite than I could have possibly imagined, Fiona," he whispered. He kept his hands to his sides.

She knew she radiated embarrassed heat, but there was more than just embarrassment there. She wanted him so badly but wasn't sure what to do next. It was one thing to study the reproduction of Homo sapiens in an anatomy textbook. She certainly understood the mechanics of mating. What she didn't know was how to go about it without inflicting or receiving pain.

"Please," she whispered, running her hand from his chest to his groin, allowing her fingers to brush over his mind-boggling erection. She could feel his body quivering.

"Please what?" he asked, sounding a little amused.

"I don't know what to do next."

He groaned and turned toward her. "Why doesn't that surprise me? What do you want to do, Fiona? I need to know so that there's no chance of misunderstanding. Not now. We've come too far.''

She swallowed. ''I want to make love with you.'' Her hand continued to slide over his skin, which had grown damp. The chill of the room didn't appear to affect him in the least.

He caught his breath when her hand daintily stroked over and around his groin area. ''I can't tell you how glad I am to hear you say that because I don't think I have the strength to turn away from you at the moment, despite all my best intentions.''

She smiled. ''You sound almost as nervous as I feel.''

He nodded, pulling her down to him, so that her head rested on his arm. He molded her to his body, making her heart pick up its beat. ''Of course I'm nervous,'' he whispered, kissing her quickly on her mouth, her eyes, her nose and her cheeks. ''It's been a while and I'm not at all sure I have enough control to love you without scaring you to death.''

''I'm not afraid of you,'' she said, looking into his eyes and his soul.

''You should be,'' he muttered, before he rolled onto his back, holding her in place. He quickly removed her bra and panties and then lifted her enough to gain access to her breasts. His mouth covered first one, then the other, tugging on the nipples until she thought she would cry out with pleasure.

She leaned over him, her legs sliding to either

side of his hips, and kissed any portion of his body she could reach. Somehow she wanted to be able to give him the same pleasure that he offered her.

He ran his hand down her back and around to her side before slipping it between their bodies. She started at the unfamiliar touch. He let go of her breast and kissed her mouth before saying, "It's all right. I won't hurt you. I promise."

He touched her intimately, his fingers moving into her body. She was embarrassed to be so damp there, but he didn't appear to mind. In a sudden move he reversed their position so that she now rested on the bed and he was on his knees between her legs. The movement of his magical fingers brought her hips off the bed to push against him, wanting him to continue his rhythmic caresses.

He must have read her mind because he didn't slow down. Instead, he moved faster and faster until she stiffened and cried out, her body no longer in her control, as she felt the most exquisite sensations pulsing through her.

He paused and looked down at her with a smile so tender she fought the tears that threatened to appear.

"Yes," he whispered. "Your eyes change color when you're making love, just as I imagined." He leaned down and captured her mouth with a possessiveness that took her breath away. This kiss was nothing like the one they had exchanged earlier—had it only been two nights ago? This time he allowed her to feel his passion, the strength of his constraint, his hunger and his need.

When he lifted his head she felt that her body had liquefied.

"I can stop now, if you want," he said, his voice strained.

"But that isn't fair to you, is it?" she asked, puzzled by his comment.

"This isn't about fair, little one. This is about what you want, remember? You're seducing me."

"Oh!" She smiled and wrapped her arms around his neck. "Then I don't want you to stop," she said, running her tongue over his ear.

This time she heard the groan that she had only felt earlier.

"Hold on," he said, and grabbed the pants that he'd thrown over the bedpost. He fished his wallet out of the back pocket with shaking hands, pulled out a small foil-wrapped package and dropped the wallet on the bed.

"I hope to hell this thing works. It's been in there longer than I can remember."

He quickly covered himself, then nudged her legs so they widened. He looked so serious, so strained and so intent that she didn't want to do or say anything to distract him.

"Let me know if I hurt you," he said, his voice husky.

She slid her arms around his neck once again,

holding him close. She closed her eyes and waited, praying it wouldn't hurt too much.

She felt him nudge her there between her legs, but this time she knew it wasn't his fingers wanting to gain entry. Reflexively she drew her knees up, cradling him between them.

He made a sound of approval before he carefully pushed himself closer to her.

He is huge, was her first thought. He'll never fit there, was her second. She reminded herself that he'd promised to stop if she hurt too badly to allow him entrance. She wanted to do this for him. He'd brought her to the most beautiful climax she could have ever imagined.

Fiona forced herself to relax.

The dampness made his entry smooth and he rocked gently over her, moving a little deeper with each small thrust before pulling away. Fiona was surprised at the teasing sensations she felt. In an effort to increase them, she lifted her hips and met his next thrust, moving him deeper with surprisingly little pain.

She didn't want Greg to slow down, to take it easy, to carefully breach the barrier. With that in mind, the next time he rocked forward, she thrust as hard as she could with her hips, using her heels to push her higher. She felt something inside her give way before he was firmly embedded inside her.

He was panting, his breathing harsh in her ear.

"I think I've died and gone to heaven," he said on a sigh.

"I didn't think it would fit," she said shyly into his ear.

"Believe me, I had the same concern. You are so small I was afraid I'd do permanent damage."

She kissed his cheek, feeling the perspiration trickle down his face.

"Now what?" she asked, and she felt his body shake with suppressed laughter.

In the next few minutes he showed her in several pleasurable ways what happened next. He made love to her with his whole body. He kept his rhythm slow while he kissed her, his tongue moving to the thrusting rhythm of his body. Fiona had never imagined such an erotic sensation.

She'd wanted this without knowing how it would feel. Now she was receiving so much pleasure that her panting moans were in counterpoint to his.

She felt herself tightening around him, the sensations that had swept over her earlier returning with more intensity than she could have imagined possible.

His movements quickened and his breathing became more labored. Fiona wrapped her arms and legs around him, unwilling to let him go.

A sudden burst of release exploded inside her, her body convulsively contracting.

Greg gathered her tightly to him and lunged

deep inside her, crying out as he reached his release. It went on and on and her body responded by contracting around him.

He rolled onto his side without letting her go, her face buried in his chest. She turned her head, gasping for air, while his heart pounded beneath her ear.

Fiona sighed with contentment and closed her eyes.

A few minutes passed before he moved, reluctantly withdrawing from her. He got out of bed, slipped on his robe and left the room. She followed his progress with her mind's eye. She heard the bathroom door close, water running, the toilet flush, more water, and then silence before she heard the door open again. She waited.

It took him longer to return to the bedroom. When he did, he had the sexiest smile on his face, which made her want to leap into his arms immediately and have her way with him again.

"Are you aware that there's food sitting on your table? I would imagine it to be cold food by now."

She had rolled to her back and pulled the covers to her chin when he'd left, feeling the chill of the room once more. She nodded. "Yes, I came in to tell you I had a meal ready."

He shook his head and chuckled. In a couple of long strides he arrived at the side of the bed. "Thank you for sharing that information with me, Miss MacDonald." He slid his hand beneath the covers and cupped her breast. "Would you like me to fetch your robe so that you can join me for dinner, late though it may be?"

With all the dignity she could muster, and it was difficult since she wanted to laugh with sheer pleasure, she nodded. "Please," she replied, in her aunt Minnie's regal tone.

He straightened, still smiling, and left the room again. This time he wasted no time returning to her, her robe in hand.

With dignified aplomb, Greg bowed and said, "Your robe, madam."

Suddenly feeling shy and more than a little wanton, she pulled the robe around her before she threw the covers off.

He shook his head, but did not comment.

Their dinner did not look nearly as appetizing now as it had when she'd first placed the dishes on the table. With quiet efficiency she reheated each item, this time making them each a plate. When both plates were filled, she returned to the table where Greg sat, watching her.

She placed the plates on the table and sat down. Without quite meeting his eye, she began to eat and noticed that he didn't waste much time diving into his meal, either.

This making-love business burned up a lot of energy, Fiona thought. Being ever practical, she decided she would stoke up on fuel just in case he might be interested in more activity before the night was over.

After the dishes were done, Fiona excused herself and went upstairs to shower. She could catch the scent of his aftershave on her once in a while and she wished she could leave it as a reminder. Maybe she wouldn't wash his pillowcase. Instead, she would keep it near her at night as a reminder of the American who had stolen her heart.

The shower door abruptly opened and she squealed in shock. Greg stood there, wearing nothing more than his smile. "May I join you?" he asked, stepping into the shower with her before she could find her tongue. "Here, I'll wash your back for you." He took the soap and washcloth from her limp hand and carefully turned her so that she stood with her back to him. He gently scrubbed her back, lifting her wet hair from her shoulders and running both hands along her hips and thighs and back up to her derriere.

When he slipped his hand around to the thatch of curls between her thighs, she was whimpering with need.

He pulled her snugly against him, then lifted her so that he could rub his erection against her bottom, teasing her with his movements until she was ready to attack him.

Greg must have known the moment when she couldn't take any more because he lowered her feet to the floor, sluiced the soap bubbles off and turned off the water. He stepped out of the shower and before she could regain her equilibrium he wrapped her in one of the bath towels and carried her into her bedroom.

Dark had descended sometime when she wasn't aware of anything other than Greg. He'd turned back her covers and had the small lamp by her bed on. While he sensuously rubbed the towel over her, he said, "I've fed McTavish and Tiger, let McTavish out for his nightly check and then let him back in and banked the fire."

"Oh?" she said weakly.

"Uh-huh. I figured after the long day we had, we probably needed to go to bed earlier than usual." He rearranged her on the bed, quickly dried himself off and knelt between her legs once again. Fiona was quickly discovering that she found that position most pleasing.

He began to massage her, starting with her neck and shoulders, her breasts—his hands teasing and tantalizing her—her waist and her abdomen until she could no longer lie still. It was when he kissed her on her abdomen and again on her thick curls that she froze.

"What are you doing?"

He glanced up, his eyes dancing. "Doing my best to further your education, Miss Fiona. Lie back and enjoy it, okay?"

"But—" she began before she forgot what she'd been about to say.

He licked her, his tongue probing into her most personal place. There had been no mention of that in the textbooks she'd read!

His fingers danced along her thighs and abdomen before moving inside once again, following the same rhythm set by his tongue.

She gave herself up to the sensations, allowing her body to build and build into an ever-tightening knot deep inside until she erupted once again, her hips pushing against him, willing him to come inside her.

When he didn't, she opened her eyes and looked at him with the question in her eyes.

"You're going to be sore in the morning, sprite. I don't want to overdo."

She wanted to tell him to please overdo if it always felt like this, but she didn't.

"I'm in rather short supply of protection, I'm afraid. So I—"

She smiled at him, causing him to blink. "I happen to have some downstairs. There are times when I seem to be one of the main suppliers in the village. Some of the married women are too shy to ask the druggist."

He closed his eyes for a moment and swallowed. When he opened them, they had darkened to a familiar hue, silently alerting her that he wouldn't be averse to the idea. "Where?" was all he said, sounding hoarse.

She sat up and slipped off the bed. She picked

up her robe and looked back at him as she went out the door. "Don't move. I'll be right back."

He wasted no time when she returned and he had her pinned to the bed in no more than a few minutes. She enthusiastically cooperated. She explored him as he had her, bringing him to the brink of climax before she slipped the protection over him and guided him inside her.

There were no gentle movements, no softly whispered words this time. Their coming together was explosive, physical and earthy. Once there, he continued his long thrusts and her hips met him, her body glistening with perspiration. When he collapsed against her she smiled, feeling quite pleased with herself. She had managed to get the hang of lovemaking with surprising ease.

Fiona knew, of course, that she would never share this intimacy with another man.

As she drifted into sleep, she drowsily hoped that Aunt Minnie had been able to enjoy such pleasure with her Robbie before he was killed. If so, it would explain why she'd never been interested in another man.

Chapter Eleven

Fiona stirred several hours later and sleepily reached for Greg, wanting to know he was real and not some figment of her overheated imagination.

He wasn't there.

She opened her eyes and looked around the room. Greg must have turned off the lamp at some point during the evening. Now the only light came from the window, where Greg stood in silhouette with his shoulder leaning against the window frame. He wore his robe and had his hands in his pockets.

"What's wrong?" she asked softly, not wanting to startle him.

He turned his head, but with the light behind him, his face was shadowed. "I didn't mean to wake you."

"You didn't. Will you talk to me…please?"

He stood there in silence long enough for Fiona to decide he wasn't going to respond before he slowly straightened and walked over to her side of the bed. He sat at the end of the bed, facing her.

Fiona knew something was terribly wrong. He'd been warm and so passionate with her, making her feel as if no one else existed for him except her. Was he already regretting their lovemaking?

She sat up and pulled her knees to her chest.

"What do you want me to say?" he finally asked.

"What were you thinking, standing there at the window?"

He gave his head a quick shake. "So many things. I couldn't begin to sort through them and make any kind of sense."

Greg sounded sad and resigned. She leaned toward him so that she could touch his hand, needing the contact.

"Are you sorry for what happened this evening?" she finally asked when he said no more.

He turned and gripped her hand as though unable to resist touching her again. "Sorry?" he repeated in a strangled voice. "That's such a mild word for what I'm feeling at the moment."

She moved closer to him. "Please don't blame

yourself for what happened, Greg. If I hadn't been so—''

''Don't blame yourself for what happened. I'm surprised it didn't happen sooner. The tension between us was palpable. Even your aunt recognized it.''

''Then what is it? Why are you awake?''

Greg was quiet for a few moments and then he sighed heavily. ''I don't like the feeling that I'm using you for my own needs without regard for your best interests. I've said more than once that I don't want to take advantage of you and I'm afraid I have.''

''Then you *are* sorry we made love. Even though I was the one who seduced you.''

His mouth flickered into a brief smile at her words. He lowered his head and kissed her so tenderly she felt her bones melt. Regardless of the turmoil he was experiencing, his gentle touch told its own tale.

Fiona slipped her arms around his shoulders and held him. By the time he released her they were both trembling.

Greg rested his forehead against hers. ''Probably none of this is real. I'm probably still hallucinating and when I wake up, none of this will have happened. Only in my dreams.'' He swallowed before saying, ''In so many ways that I can't explain, I almost wish this were only a dream. You see, it doesn't change anything. You need to know that. It doesn't change a thing.''

''I know. If wasn't supposed to change anything. It just happened, that's all. I don't regret it. I don't want you to, either.''

''I had no business—'' he began before her fingers stopped him.

''Let's don't waste time when you only have a few more hours here,'' she whispered. ''There's to be no recriminations, remember? Just pleasure. Let's enjoy the pleasure.''

He removed his robe, returned to bed and made tender love to her, his gentleness bringing tears to her eyes.

When Greg opened his eyes several hours later, he saw daylight filtering through the window. He glanced at Fiona who lay next to him, her hand resting on his chest.

A soft scratching at the door caught his attention and he recognized the noise that had awakened him. Moving carefully in an effort not to wake up Fiona, Greg quickly dressed and went to the door. He wasn't surprised to see McTavish sitting there, looking abandoned and bereft.

Without a word, Greg went downstairs and quickly fed both animals before letting them outside. Then he went into the downstairs bathroom and prepared for his day.

After his shower and shave, Greg went to his

room. It took only a few minutes for him to repack his belongings. After taking a careful look around, he returned to the hallway and set his suitcase by the door.

He went back upstairs and found Fiona still sleeping. He knew he had exhausted her the night before. He hadn't been able to leave her alone. He'd told himself that his reaction was due to the three years he'd gone without sex.

This morning he knew differently, but his knowledge of his motives didn't change the facts. He had other commitments that did not include the young woman before him.

He pulled out the small notebook that he always carried in his pocket, wrote a brief note and left it on the pillow he'd slept on the night before.

Once downstairs, he stepped out the back door and whistled for McTavish who eagerly dashed toward him. Greg squatted on his haunches in front of the dog.

"I'm leaving you in charge. Take care of her, all right? You stay close and make certain she's safe." He opened the back door and followed McTavish. He watched him climb the stairs and nudge the bedroom door open before disappearing inside.

After a moment, Greg picked up his suitcase and let himself out the front door.

He had several hours of driving to do before he reached Glasgow. He would check into a hotel near the airport to be ready for his flight home. He kept his mind carefully blank of everything but what he was doing. He wanted no memories of any kind to distract him.

He was going home. That was all that mattered.

Fiona was drowsily aware of Greg's weight in her bed. He hadn't left yet, she thought with a smile. She knew he would need to go soon, but for now, she could pretend that he was staying in Scotland with her.

Without opening her eyes, she reached for him. Startled, her eyes flew open and she sat up in bed, staring at McTavish, who lay stretched out beside her.

''What do you think you're doing?'' she asked with a mixture of disappointment and amusement. ''You know you aren't supposed to sleep on the bed!''

McTavish thumped the bed with his tail.

Fiona looked around the room, knowing without need for confirmation that Greg had left. She looked at the clock and was startled to see it was almost ten o'clock. No doubt Greg had been gone for hours.

She tossed the covers back, got up and headed for the bathroom. Once under the warm spray from the shower, she allowed her emotions free rein. Only she would know the amount of tears she shed that morning while the water washed them away.

By the time she dried off and dressed, she was once again in control. She had her own life, after all. She had always known that he would leave. There never had been a reason for him to stay.

She wasn't sorry for experiencing lovemaking with him. No matter how he wanted to look at what had happened, she was fully aware that he had been touched by what they had shared, even if he hadn't admitted it.

At least she had had those few hours with him when he had let down his emotional barriers and had allowed her close to him. He'd allowed her to see his vulnerability as well as his inability to let anyone get close to him on a permanent basis. Otherwise she wouldn't have found him awake in the middle of the night concerned about what had happened between them.

McTavish had gone downstairs by the time she returned to her bedroom. She stripped the sheets off her bed and replaced them with clean ones, before making up the bed.

As she turned away, she noticed a folded piece of paper lying on the floor. She picked it up and opened it, then slowly sat on the side of the bed.

She'd never seen Greg's handwriting before. She was struck by the bold strokes and lack of frills, so much like the man himself.

"Fiona," she read, "I couldn't force myself to wake you this morning so I'm taking the coward's way out and telling you goodbye this way. There's no way I can repay what you have done for me. Please take care of yourself.'' It was simply signed ''Greg.''

Tears trickled down her cheeks once again, but she refused to give in to them. Not now. Not ever. What was done was done and could not be changed, even if she wished it so. Which she did not. She touched her still-tender lips with her fingertips and whispered, ''I will never forget you, Greg Dumas. That is my blessing and my curse.''

Greg was one of the first to board the plane back to the States early the next morning. He hadn't slept much the night before, despite being tired from the long drive from Glen Cairn.

When he finally had fallen asleep, he'd dreamed about Jill, which wasn't unusual, and yet these dreams were different. They weren't about her death. They were about his explaining to her why he had made love to another woman.

He kept waking up, feeling like the worst kind of heel. Once awake, he still couldn't rid himself of the guilt of becoming involved with another woman.

Once buckled into his seat, he closed his eyes and waited for the plane to take off. He reminded himself that the only wrong he'd committed was against Fiona, not against Jill.

He'd taken the gift Fiona had offered, knowing that he had little to give in return. She'd been generous and loving and he'd wanted to protect her from her own impetuous choices. But he hadn't. Instead, he'd taken full advantage of the situation.

Greg didn't like the view he saw of himself every time he closed his eyes.

By the time the plane left Glasgow, Greg was asleep. He slept most of the way to New York. When the plane landed several hours later, he was ready to face the day with a minimum of jet lag.

Jill's parents and Tina met him when he came out of Customs. Tina raced to him and threw herself into his arms, chattering all the while she kissed him all over the face, from his brows to his chin.

Helen laughingly gave him a hug and George shook his hand, but it wasn't until they returned home that Greg was able to say much about the trip.

Over a late lunch he told them about Scotland. He'd already given Tina the souvenirs he'd picked up for her and she had what seemed like hundreds of questions about everything.

It was later that afternoon when he called his client to report on his lack of success. When the phone was answered, he heard, "MacLeod residence."

"May I speak with Ms. MacLeod, please? This is Greg Dumas."

"Ah, yes, Mr. Dumas. I'm Janet O'Reilly, Ms.

MacLeod's housekeeper. She mentioned that you might call while she's away.''

"She's not here?"

"No, she's in Italy at the moment. I'm not certain where, exactly. If it's urgent I can give you telephone numbers to try.''

"I don't think it's urgent enough to disturb her in Italy. Would you please have her call me when she returns?"

"Certainly, Mr. Dumas.'' He gave her his number and hung up.

So that took care of that. He'd go to the office tomorrow and type up a report. He preferred to tell her in person about the possibility that Fiona was her sister. He wondered if Mr. McCloskey would confirm that Fiona was one of the triplets. That would be something for Ms. MacLeod to handle.

That night Helen suggested that both he and Tina stay with them rather than return home for the night. Greg didn't care one way or the other so let Tina choose. Now that he was home, Tina was comfortable staying one more night at her grandparents' home before returning to her former routine with her father.

Once Tina was in bed, Helen said, "So tell me what you haven't told us," she said, her eyes twinkling with amusement.

Greg looked at her in surprise, while George made a disgusted sound behind the paper he was reading.

"I don't know what you're talking about."

Helen grinned. "All right. Then I'll be more specific. You haven't mentioned a word about Fiona. I want to hear more about her."

"C'mon, Helen. I told you before. She was kind enough to look after me when I fell sick. When I was better, it made sense that I stay there while going through her father's files, for all the good that did me."

"You said she was twenty-five. Tall, short, blonde, brunette? What is she like?"

Greg sighed and ran his hand through his hair. "She's small...not just short...but slender, as well. Her hair is red."

Helen waited, and when he said no more, said, "And you were attracted to her, right?"

George lowered the paper. "Leave the man alone, will ya, Helen? Can't he have any secrets?"

Helen ignored her spouse. "I can hear it in your voice. I can't tell you how relieved I am."

"Relieved," Greg repeated slowly.

"For the past three years you've buried yourself in your work. Outside of Tina, and us, of course, you've made no effort to stay in touch with friends or do anything else. Work is not the answer for what ails you, Greg. I hope you've begun to understand that."

Greg shook his head. "I have a life, Helen. I stay busy. I have a daughter whom I love very much. What more do I need?"

"A woman in your life."

He pinched the bridge of his nose. "That sounds strange, coming from you."

"Why? Because I'm Jill's mother? Well, she'd be telling you the same thing if she were able to express herself at the moment. And you know what? She'd be right. Grieving is one thing. We've all done that. But life goes on. Tina is growing up. Your company has taken off. Now it's time for you to slow down a little and meet new people."

"What does any of this have to do with Fiona?"

"That's what I'm asking you, you thickheaded cop. Something happened to you over there, besides this case you're working on, and I'm betting that something was Fiona MacDonald. Now you tell me if I'm wrong."

"You're wrong," he replied doggedly.

"Ha!" Helen replied.

"There," George said. "He answered you. Now leave him alone."

Helen threw up her hands. "All right, if that's the way you want it. I just figured you might want someone to talk to, someone who would understand, but if you want to keep everything all bottled up, like you've done for the past three years, why, be my guest!" She turned and walked out of the room.

"Women," George muttered.

Greg smiled. "But we can't get along without them," Greg replied.

George gave him a penetrating look. "You know Helen means well. She worries about you. We both do."

Greg stood and walked over to George in his recliner. He patted George on the shoulder. "Thanks. I appreciate both of you more than I can ever tell you."

Greg wandered over to the piano, where Helen had arranged family photographs. He stood and looked at the display, his hands in his pockets.

Jill smiled at him from her various school pictures, her graduation snapshots and while she held a newborn Tina at the hospital.

Jill had been a beautiful person, inside and out. Tall and voluptuous, with dark curly hair and exotic features. Her smile had been the first thing he'd noticed about her—that, and her vivacious personality.

Standing there, he remembered how she used to give him a bad time about being such a sourpuss. She'd probably been right. He knew that he'd laughed more in the five years he'd known Jill than he had during the first twenty-five years of his miserable life.

He shook his head and turned away.

Greg left the room after bidding George goodnight. He went into the guest bedroom where he undressed and crawled into bed, still wide-awake. He rested his head on his folded arms and remembered....

His mother died when Greg was eight and he'd been raised—if that was the word—by a father who got mean when he was drunk…and he was never sober.

By the time he left home, Greg had bailed his dad out of jail for drunkenness too many times to feel anything more than contempt for him. Once he left, Greg never went back.

He had no idea whether his father was dead or alive.

He'd put himself through school and joined the police department when he was twenty-one. He'd worked hard for his promotions and by the time Jill showed up in his life four years later, he'd made sergeant.

She'd been hired as a civilian to work at his precinct and help with the endless paperwork. They got married that first year and Tina came along three years later. He'd been cocky back then, and why not? He'd had everything he ever wanted in life—a good job, a beautiful wife, a nice home in a quiet neighborhood and a precious daughter.

Tina was two the night they'd left her with Helen and George while they caught a movie. He could still see Jill as she looked that night—the dress she wore, the way she'd fixed her hair.

After the movie, they'd left the theater and strolled down the street, chatting about the show. Jill had cried at the sappy ending, he remembered, and he was teasing her about being so sentimental.

They had passed a convenience store and Jill reminded him they were almost out of milk, so they went inside. She went back to the dairy case while he browsed through the magazines near the front of the store.

It was while he waited that he happened to glance over at the guy behind the counter who stood frozen in place, staring at something in a customer's hand. Greg moved to get a better view and saw a punk kid in a leather jacket holding a .38.

As quietly as he could, he found Jill, handed her the cell phone and told her to get outside and report a robbery in progress. He could hear the guy be-hind the counter explaining to the kid that he didn't have access to the safe and that there was less than fifty dollars in the till.

Greg drew his weapon and waited for the patrol car to get there. He'd been unaware the kid had backup outside who must have seen Greg with his gun. The next thing Greg knew, the guy outside was spraying the store with a semiautomatic, yell-ing for his partner to run.

The patrol car arrived, sirens screaming as Greg fired back at the perp outside, taking him out. The kid at the counter ran to the back of the store but there were cops there waiting for him.

Greg remembered flashing his badge and run-ning to the front door to check on Jill. When he reached the street he saw a crowd gathered. Jill lay on the ground. One of the officers knelt beside her. A stray bullet had hit her in the neck, severing her carotid artery. There was no way to stem the bleeding.

She had died in his arms before the paramedics arrived.

Greg had lived with his guilt ever since that night. He should never have drawn his weapon. Instead, he should have grabbed Jill and gotten the hell out of there, then called the police.

Better yet, he should never have been a cop. If he'd been an accountant or a truck driver, he wouldn't have made an attempt to stop a robbery. He would have gotten his wife out and made sure she was safe.

Instead, he'd gotten her killed.

The counselors he'd been forced to see for months after her death kept telling him that it was just one of those senseless killings. That none of it had been his fault.

Even Helen had asked him how long he was going to continue to blame himself for what had happened. Now it was Helen who wanted to know what had happened to him while he'd been in Scotland.

Fiona had happened to him.

Fiona, the sprite, who had taken in a stranger and cared for him when he was out of his head with fever. Fiona, who looked so fragile and yet had so much strength.

Fiona, who, naively, was convinced she had seduced him the last night he was there.

Fiona, who had stirred something inside of him that he'd thought was dead.

Now he had two women haunting him, one who would never return, the other too far away and much too different ever to become a part of his life.

Not that he would want her in his life. He never wanted to feel so vulnerable again. The pain and sense of loss was something he never again wanted to experience.

So he had left without explaining any of his life to Fiona. He had no reason ever to return.

When Greg finally fell asleep, he dreamed of Jill again. She came to him and held him, trying to comfort him. When he tried to explain, she shook her head and smiled. She looked happy. She said she wanted him to know that she had no regrets. She loved him. What she wanted for him was happiness. True happiness.

"It's time to let go of me," she whispered. "I'm fine. You must go on without me."

With a final kiss, she turned and walked away from him, growing smaller and smaller until she disappeared.

Chapter Twelve

Greg left the subway and strode the blocks necessary to reach the restaurant where he was to meet with Kelly MacLeod. He'd been back in New York for two weeks. Instead of settling into his comfortable and familiar routine, he'd found himself becoming more and more restless.

Erotic dreams of Fiona had him waking each morning in a trembling state of arousal. He felt as though her presence had taken over his life. He found himself reaching for the phone at odd hours wanting to call her just to hear her voice.

When Kelly MacLeod had returned his call yesterday, he was reminded of Fiona's lilting voice, even though Ms. MacLeod's voice had no hint of a Scottish accent.

Now he was going to meet her in order to tell her the final piece of news that he had not put into his report.

As soon as he walked into the restaurant, he saw her sitting near one of the windows. As the light hit her, he could immediately see the same heart-shaped face, the long slender neck and the slight build of the woman who had haunted his dreams.

When Ms. MacLeod turned and looked at him, the differences between them were more apparent. His client's eyes were a deep blue, not sea-green. Her hair, although as silky as Fiona's, was a light blond without a hint of red.

He pulled out a chair and sat down. "I hope I haven't kept you waiting," he said.

She smiled, but her eyes betrayed a sadness that hadn't been there when he had first met her. Or maybe he hadn't noticed back then.

"Would you like to look at the menu and order?" she asked. "I was early so I already know what I want."

Once their orders were taken and their beverages brought to the table, he said, "I have something to tell you that wasn't in my report."

"Oh? About Douglas and Moira?"

"No. Unfortunately, I ran out of leads where they were concerned. The attorney gave me additional information that I believe you have the right to know.''

''Which is?''

''You were one of three girls born that night…and I believe I know where one of your sisters lives.''

Kelly stared at him in disbelief. ''Are you saying that I was one of triplets?''

He nodded.

''And we weren't kept together?''

''According to the attorney, he and the doctor felt the only way to protect the three of you was to separate you.''

''Because of the relative my mother was running from,'' she said thoughtfully.

''That's correct.''

''You say you know where one of them is? But not both?''

''I kept my search limited to your parents. Just before I left Scotland, I discovered from a relative of the doctor who delivered you that he had adopted a girl who shares the same birthdate as you. I believe that his daughter, Fiona MacDonald, is your sister.''

''And you told her this?''

He shook his head. ''It wasn't my place to tell her. You are my client. Therefore, I am giving you the information to do with as you please.''

Kelly leaned back in her chair. ''A sister,'' she said a little breathlessly. ''I have sisters I never knew about.'' She closed her eyes. ''My life is becoming stranger by the hour.''

Their meals were brought and they ate without discussing his news. Over coffee, Kelly said, ''Tell me about Fiona MacDonald. Did you actually see her?''

''Not only did I see her, I stayed at her home for almost a week. I arrived there sick and she nursed me back to health.''

Her lips twitched. ''That sounds terribly romantic, you know,'' she said. He knew that she was teasing but he couldn't control his embarrassed reaction. When she saw him squirm, she said, ''Ah, perhaps it was more romantic than I thought. Please tell me more.''

''Uh, not really. I understand I wasn't a very docile patient.''

Her eyes widened. ''Imagine that,'' she said with a chuckle.

Greg understood his client's need to find out more about Fiona, so he began to tell her about the cottage, about McTavish and Tiger, about Fiona. He must have gotten carried away because he seemed to talk forever before he finally ran down.

She had listened carefully, her chin resting on her clasped hands, while he had described the area, the people and his stay there. She said nothing when he finished, which further embarrassed him. No doubt he'd given her much more information than she had either wanted or needed to hear.

The waiter refilled their cups. Once he walked away, she said, "You're in love with her."

He frowned. "Of course not. She was just a woman who—"

She waved her hand, stopping him. "I'm very much aware that 'she was just a woman who.' You're a very observant man, Mr. Dumas, and you are meticulous in recalling all that you saw. That goes without saying. You wouldn't be as successful as you are without it. And you came highly recommended when I was looking for someone to handle this matter for me.

"It isn't what you said. It's how you said it. Even the way you say her name. So don't deny it, Mr. Dumas. Whether you intended to keep it a secret or not, the fact is, you're in love with her. If it makes you feel better, your secret is safe with me." Her gamine grin reminded him so much of Fiona that he felt the pain of loss more sharply than usual.

"Well, it doesn't matter," he finally said gruffly. "I just thought you would want to know something about her."

"Oh, I do. And I've been thinking. I have some free time on my hands. I'd like to go to Scotland and meet my sister and perhaps the attorney, as well. And I now have a new assignment for you. I want you to find my other sister, as well as introduce me to the one you found."

"You don't need me for that, Ms. MacLeod,"

he said hurriedly. "I'm sure that you can explain—"

"But since you know her so much better," she said slyly, "it would make more sense for you to break the news to her that we're related before we actually meet, don't you think?"

Greg was beyond thinking at the moment. How had he managed to reveal such strong feelings for a person whom he had every intention of forgetting?

"I'm willing to pay you anything you ask if you'll go with me to Scotland and handle this matter for me."

He stared at her in dismay. She was absolutely serious. He could see that. He didn't really blame her. She'd been looking for birth family. Even though she hadn't found what she had expected, there was family there for her.

"I won't take your money, Ms. MacLeod, but if you insist, I'll take you to Scotland and introduce you to Mr. McCloskey and Ms. MacDonald."

"Ahh. It's Ms. MacDonald, is it? Well, whatever you choose to call her, I hope you will prepare her for the shock of finding that she has a sister."

"There will be another shock, as well. She was told that she was adopted because she was the niece of Mrs. MacDonald. Discovering that they lied to her will be disturbing."

"Really! Then that will give us something more in common, won't it?" She glanced at her watch.

"I'll see about getting reservations for us, Mr. Dumas, and regardless of your chivalrous offer, I intend to pay you for your time and expenses." Kelly stood and adjusted the strap of her purse over her shoulder.

"I'm glad you didn't put this bit of news into the report. Knowing you, you wouldn't have given me *all* the details that you've provided over lunch."

He stopped himself from rolling his eyes. "I'm afraid you're reading too much into my verbal report, Ms. MacLeod."

She smiled. "Am I? Well, we'll see, won't we?"

Greg let himself into the Santini home, already dreading to tell Helen that he would be returning to Scotland. On his way back to Queens he kept going over what Kelly had said to him. His thoughts didn't do much for his mood. By the time he walked into the house, he felt so frustrated and irritable that he wondered if he shouldn't have gone on home first.

"It's me," he called out, heading toward the kitchen, the center of activity for the family.

Helen was putting the finishing touches on the top crust of a cherry pie when he walked into the room. She looked at him in surprise. "Did my clock stop or are you early today?"

He glanced at his watch. "I'm early," he said

shortly, and helped himself to a cup of coffee. He sat on one of the chairs near a wall and tipped it back on two legs, staring at nothing.

Helen slipped the pie into the oven, set the timer, poured herself a cup of coffee and sat down across the table from him. "Bad day?" she suggested.

He dropped the chair and set the cup on the table. "Yeah. A bad day, a bad week, a bad month."

"Is it something you want to talk about?" she asked with sympathy.

He leaned his forearms on the table and stared down at the coffee. "Yeah, because you need to know."

She folded her hands on the table and waited. She knew that sooner or later he'd find the words to express what he was feeling. He'd never been good at expressing himself, particularly when his emotions were involved. She hadn't seen him so edgy in a long while.

He glanced at her, then away. "Have you ever heard this advice about listening to other people? If someone comes up to you and comments on your tail, you can ignore him because you know damn well you don't have a tail. If a second person comes along and makes some remark about your tail…you might wonder why people are commenting on something that doesn't exist. However, if a third person mentions it, you'd better turn around and look. There's a good chance you have a tail, whether you know it or not."

Helen smiled. "Good advice, I would think. So did you just discover you have a tail?"

He groaned and rubbed his hand over his face. "Worse. Much worse. I finally realized—after Minnie MacDonald, you and Kelly MacLeod pointed it out to me—that I'm in love with Fiona MacDonald." He picked up his cup and drained it.

Helen smiled. "And that disturbs you?"

"Hell, yes, it disturbs me! Why shouldn't it? How could I have been so unaware of my feelings for her, so convinced that the attraction wasn't anything that could become permanent even when I've been unable to get her out of mind?"

"I take it that Kelly MacLeod asked about Fiona."

He sighed. "Yeah. She asked me to tell her about Fiona. So I did. That's all. I just told her what I'd observed and learned about her. Kelly accused me of being in love...and she doesn't even know me! Have I been so obvious to everybody else and still didn't see it?"

"I would say that pretty well sums it up."

He played with the handle of his empty cup. "I still can't believe it. How could I let myself fall for somebody that lives on the other side of the Atlantic? The whole idea is ridiculous." The heat had gone out of his voice.

"We don't always have control over who we fall in love with, you know. If we did, I would never have married George Santini!" She chuckled at some memory from the past. "What do you intend to do about it?"

He looked up from his intent absorption in the cup and Helen had a glimpse of what he was going through.

"I don't know," he answered quietly. "I honestly don't know. I mean, look at the whole thing sensibly. Our lives are so different…our culture is different…I know she would hate living here, but how can I move there?" He gave his head a quick shake. "That's assuming, of course, that she feels the same way, which is far from certain."

He thought of the last night they'd spent together and how she had clung to him, responding to him with complete abandon, encouraging him to continue to make love to her through most of the night.

Was that when it first happened that he slipped from being attracted to her into this all-consuming, nerve-wracking obsession he seemed to have developed. He couldn't sleep without dreaming of her. She was on his mind so much, he was distracted most of the time whether he was at home or working.

"Have you discussed any of this with Tina?" Helen asked, breaking the silence that had fallen.

"Of course not! She wouldn't understand at all."

"You might be surprised. Tina doesn't remember Jill, you know. I leave Jill's photographs around the house so that she will have some idea what her mother was like. She asks questions, sometimes, but what I see is a little girl who wants a mother in her life, someone young like the other children's parents.''

''I didn't know.''

''That's because she doesn't want to hurt your feelings. She loves her daddy. He just can't take the place of a mother. Does Fiona know about Tina?''

He nodded. ''I can't believe I'm in this situation. We only knew each other a week or so.''

''You told me you knew that you wanted Jill the first time you saw her.''

His lips curved into a slight smile. ''Well, yeah, but I'm not sure that was love.''

She wrinkled her nose. ''Okay, it was lust at first sight on your part, but it quickly developed into much more.''

''I know.'' He got up and got another cup of coffee, refilling Helen's cup, as well. Once he was seated, he said, ''I don't want to go through that again, Helen.''

''Falling in love? I believe it's been established as having already happened.''

''I don't want to go through the pain and sense of loss I went through when we lost Jill, Helen. It hurts too much.''

''I understand about being vulnerable, Greg. The fact is that whenever we love another person, we're vulnerable. It's part of life's experiences. That doesn't mean we stop loving. That's the same as to stop living. If something happens to a loved one and we lose them, there's nothing we can do except to grieve the loss and go on.'' She reached across the table and rested her hand on top of his. ''You've dwelt on the downside of love long enough. It's time for you to enjoy the upside—the joy of being with the one you love. We both know that life is too uncertain not to cherish every moment we are with a loved one.

''It's time for you to go after what you want, Greg,'' Helen continued. ''That's one of the many traits I've admired about you—your tenacity. You've never let anything stand in your way.''

He looked at her, his gaze bleak. ''I've started to call Fiona a half-dozen times since I got home, but I never had the nerve. When I left, I said nothing about returning…and now I'm going back, like it or not.''

''Really? Did your client ask you to return?''

He nodded. ''She wants to meet Fiona. And she wants to find out what happened to the third sister. So she's going over as soon as she can arrange everything and wants me there to introduce them.''

''There you go. A perfect opportunity to see Fiona again.''

The front door slammed and racing steps echoed in the hallway. ''Daddy, you're here!'' Tina said, charging into the room and barreling into him. He lifted her onto his lap and gave her a kiss and a hug.

"How was school?" he asked.

"Bor-rring," she replied. "But you know what? One of the mommies brought everyone cookies so we had a party."

"Well, good for you."

Tina glanced at Helen. "Maybe sometime could you bring something for us?"

"You bet. Just tell me when." She looked past Tina at Greg and said, "Your daddy has some exciting news for you."

Tina turned and looked at him. "Really?"

Greg took a deep breath and made the plunge. "I need to go back to Scotland for a little while. There's a lady over there that I really like and I miss her. I'm hoping she feels the same way."

"You mean you're going to marry her?"

"I don't know. But I'm going to ask her."

"Can I go with you?"

"Not this time, but soon." He looked at Helen. "Her aunt asked me if you would be willing to move there."

Helen straightened in surprise. "Us? George and me?"

"Yeah."

"Now there's an intriguing thought. George's been talking about retiring for the past couple of years but complains that after he quits, he won't have anything to do."

Thinking aloud, Greg said, "I'm going to look into opening a branch office in Edinburgh. I could use George in the office, if he thinks it's something he'd like to do."

"So when are you leaving?"

"I don't know. My client will let me know when she has the tickets."

"Are you going to call Fiona to tell her?"

He thought about hearing her voice again, telling her what he felt, asking her to marry him. "I don't think so," he finally replied. "I want to be face-to-face with her when I tell her. She may toss me out on my ear. When I think of the way I behaved most of the time I was there, I wouldn't blame her."

Tina said, "Would this lady be my new mommy?"

"If she agrees to marry me, yes."

Tina clapped her hands. "Good. I want to have a mommy." Her gaze suddenly went to Helen. "You're a good mommy," she began, before Helen stopped her.

"No, I'm your grandmother. I'll always be your grandmother. You're absolutely right. It's time you had a real mommy. We'll hope that Fiona is willing to take on the Dumas crew…and maybe the Santinis, as well."

Chapter Thirteen

Three weeks after he left Glen Cairn, Greg was returning. He'd had better luck in finding Mr. Mc-Closkey at home this time. The solicitor confirmed that Kelly and Fiona were part of a set of triplets. Now that Kelly was there, he gave them the name of the family who adopted the third sister and their last known address. He explained that he could not ethically give out such information to anyone except the triplets themselves.

At that point Kelly sent him to Fiona to prepare her for their meeting.

He'd stopped for lunch and to fill up the rental car with gas earlier in the day. Impatient to see her again, he was on his way within the hour. By the time he reached the turnoff to Fiona's place, his heart was racing. For the past week he'd been mentally rehearsing what he would say to her, depending on her reaction to seeing him again. He was as prepared as he knew how to be, regardless of the reception he received.

Except for the one he got.

He pulled into the driveway and stopped in front of the cottage. There was no smoke coming from the chimney, which meant she must have spent most of the day in the village.

Well, he could do something about that. He knew where she kept a spare key to the back door. He could visit with McTavish until she returned home.

With his plan in place, Greg stepped out of the car, glad that he had bought a coat and boots in Edinburgh for this kind of weather. He waited for McTavish to start barking as he walked around the cottage, but there wasn't a sound. Nor was there any sign of Tiger.

He felt for the key and found it, then let himself into the kitchen.

The place was cold enough to hang meat, he thought. There was a bone-gripping cold that felt as though it had been there for days.

Greg looked around the kitchen, trying to figure out what was different. Then it hit him. The place looked bare. Outside of the usual appliances and the table and chairs, there was nothing sitting out.

He headed toward the front of the house. "McTavish? Where are you, boy?" He stopped in the doorway of the living room. The place had been stripped bare of all those things that had made it look warm and cozy. The furniture remained except for the small desk where he'd worked, but the books, the afghans, the throw rug in front of the fire and all the knickknacks that women seemed to collect were gone.

He took the stairs two at a time. The bedroom was equally bare, the bed stripped down to the mattress. He tried to think. Who could he ask about her? Then he remembered the farmer who had kept McTavish for them, Patrick McKay.

He wasted no time leaving the cottage, after he made certain it was locked again and the extra key returned to its place.

He half hoped that McTavish would greet him as he had once before, but when he pulled up, the farmyard was empty of animals. Dusk had descended since he'd first arrived at Fiona's cottage. Warm light spilled from the windows of the house while the scent of a peat fire hung in the air.

His heart pounded in his chest and he broke out in a cold sweat. The warm glow of light from the farmhouse windows and smelling the peat burning strongly reminded him of Fiona. The scent had caught him off guard, taking him back to his stay with Fiona—of keeping the fire going while he went through files, of watching the way the firelight gilded her hair. As though he'd just left her bed, he was suddenly bombarded with the scenes and sounds that surrounded them his last night with her.

Where was she? He'd been prepared to tell her everything he'd refused to discuss when he was here before. He needed to tell her how much he loved her and wanted her as a permanent part of his life.

He fought the panic that threatened to overcome him at the thought he would never be able to find her.

Greg gave his head a quick shake and got out of the car. Patrick answered the door on the first knock.

"Well, hello. It's Greg, isn't it?" Patrick asked. "I thought I heard a car outside, but when nobody got out, I thought maybe somebody had gotten lost and was using our driveway to turn around."

Lost was a good way to describe what Greg was feeling at the moment.

"Come in, come in, and get yourself warmed. Have you eaten? We still have food on the stove."

"Oh, I don't want to bother you—" was all he got out before Patrick brushed his words aside.

"Nonsense. There's always plenty. I'll have Sharon dish up a plate for you." Greg was still reeling from the unexpected cordiality of the greeting. He was even more taken aback when Patrick asked, "So how is Fiona these days? We've really missed having her here. I have to admit that McTavish has quite a way about him. Don't tell her, but I've been missing McTavish almost as much as Fiona."

Patrick had gone ahead of Greg while Greg paused to wash his hands. By the time Greg walked into the kitchen, a large bowl of stew and a slab of freshly baked bread were on the table.

"I'm looking for Fiona and I was hoping you might know where I could find her." Greg sat down and began to eat.

"Why, I thought she was with you," Patrick replied, placing a steaming mug of coffee before him.

Greg stared at him in shock. "With me? Why would you think that?"

"Well, when she told us she was leaving after you'd been gone only a few days, I figured she must have decided to go with you. You mean she didn't?"

"No. I haven't been in touch with her. She'll come back to the cottage eventually, won't she?"

"She said the cottage had served its purpose. She told me when I rented it to her that she wasn't certain how long she'd be staying. I told her at the time she could stay as long as she liked. When she told me she was leaving, she apologized for the sudden notice, but it doesn't really matter. I've got a son who'll be moving back in a couple of months. He'll be glad to have a place to stay.''

Greg felt exhausted after the long drive and the emotional gearing up to face her. Now to discover that she had disappeared was a shock.

''Well, I'm sorry you didn't know she'd moved,'' Patrick continued. ''So that's why you're here...to see Fiona.''

''Yes.''

Patrick grinned. ''I imagine she'll be pleased to see you.''

Clumsily Greg got to his feet. ''The meal was delicious and I thank you for it. Please tell your wife that I enjoyed it very much.'' He glanced at his watch. ''I don't want to seem rude, but I need to get on the road.''

''You can't be thinking about continuing your travels tonight. Why don't you spend the night with us and get an early start in the morning? We have plenty of beds around here and—if you don't mind my saying so—you look as if you could use a few hours of rest.''

Greg couldn't believe the man's generosity. He thought about arguing, but he knew Patrick was right. He wasn't ready to face another long drive at the moment.

''I appreciate the offer. You're being very generous to someone you barely know.''

Patrick stood and slapped Greg on the back. ''Nonsense. Any friend of McTavish's is a friend of mine. Come on. I'll show you where you can sleep.''

Once in bed, Greg had no trouble falling asleep. When he woke the next morning he realized that he'd slept better than he'd expected he would, or perhaps he'd been more tired than he'd realized. He would tell his hosts goodbye and get on the road. He intended to find Fiona, regardless of how long it took.

When he walked into the kitchen, Patrick and Sharon waved him to the table where a hearty breakfast awaited. An hour later, Greg waved goodbye to them as though they were longtime friends.

As soon as he was on his way, Greg's thoughts reverted to Fiona. He wanted to see her again, to hold her again, to explain to her why he had left so abruptly before, why he hadn't been able to talk to her earlier about the pain he carried. He wanted to hear her soothing voice and feel her gentle touch, see her smile and hear her laughter.

The enchanted cottage of his memory had been returned to an ordinary small house with well-used furniture and furnishings, awaiting someone else's presence to turn it into a home.

He drove to Craigmor because he had no idea where else to go. Perhaps Minnie would know where Fiona was.

There was no reason to think that anything had

happened to her, but there was enough uncertainty to make him uneasy.

By the time he reached Craigmor he'd convinced himself that Fiona would be at her aunt's home.

He pulled into the driveway of the MacDonald family residence and stopped in front of the wide stone steps. He knocked several times before Becky opened the door.

"My goodness," she exclaimed. "Look who's here! Please come in, Mr. Dumas. The weather has grown a bit nippy since your last visit, don't you think?"

He hadn't noticed, partly because his coat and hat kept him warmer, he supposed.

"I'm sorry to bother you," he began, then stopped as Becky walked away, motioning him to follow her.

"Miss Minnie will be delighted to see you. She gets lonely at this time of year, which seems strange when you think about it, considering she's lived alone for years."

Greg felt his heart sink. If Minnie MacDonald was alone, Fiona must not be here.

He paused in the doorway of Minnie's sitting room. Minnie was ensconced in one of her chairs, carefully tucked in beneath a lap robe, reading in front of the fireplace. The scene was so reminiscent of the way Fiona used to spend her evenings that he ached with the memory.

She turned her head just as Becky said, "I'll get you something warm to drink. Coffee, isn't it?" she asked. He nodded.

"Hello, Greg," Minnie said casually, as though he'd been away for no more than an hour or so. "Do come in and get warm. The winter weather seems to bring on all sorts of aches and pains to my old bones. Otherwise, I'd be up to greet you."

He slipped off his coat and cap and walked toward the fireplace.

"It's good to see you, Ms. MacDonald," he said quietly. "I hope you've been well." He sat in a nearby chair.

"Have you had lunch?" she asked, as Becky came in with a tray.

"Uh, no. I didn't bother to stop."

Becky smiled. "I'll see to it, young man. You stay right there."

Minnie poured a steaming cup of coffee for him, and filled another cup with tea for herself.

"What brings you back so soon, young man? Not that I'm not pleased to see you, but when you left you seemed to feel your investigation was over."

He warmed his hands with the hot cup while he thought about how he wanted to answer her question. He needed to tell Fiona how he felt about her before discussing the matter with anyone else, so he said, "My client wanted to come to Scotland to confirm that she and Fiona are, in fact, sisters. She asked that I escort her and introduce her to Fiona.''

''Ah. Where is your client?''

''In Edinburgh. When I explained to her that Fiona didn't know about their relationship, she thought the wisest course of action would be for me to discuss the matter with Fiona first before springing a long-lost sister on her.''

''It was thoughtful of you to come see me,'' Minnie said. ''Ever since the night you and I discussed this, I've been debating with myself about whether or not I should mention to Fiona her possible connection to your client. I couldn't decide the best course so I've ended up saying nothing to her.''

''I've just come from Glen Cairn, thinking I would find Fiona there. Since she's moved, I'm hoping that you might know where I can find her.''

Minnie sipped her tea and stared into the fireplace. She remained silent until she finished drinking and set the cup down.

''Well, it has turned out the way it needed to, I guess. I never questioned Jamie about why he made up such an elaborate story to tell everyone about Fiona's birth. The news isn't going to be easy for her to hear or accept.''

''I know.''

''Still…to find out that she has a sister might be just the thing to cheer her up. She's been in the doldrums lately.''

His pulse leapt. "Then you've spoken with her recently?"

Minnie shrugged. "Not as much as I'd like. She told me she'd been back for more than a week before she called to say she had returned to Craigmor. I still haven't talked her into coming for a visit." She looked at Greg. "She's rather a stubborn thing, in case you haven't noticed."

"I've noticed," Greg replied dryly. "I'm hoping you can tell me where's she staying."

Becky returned with another tray, this time carrying a plate of steaming food. With practiced efficiency she opened a TV tray with one hand, placed the plate on it and once she'd set the other tray down, moved the food directly in front of him.

"You're spoiling me," he said to Becky after thanking her for her trouble. When she left the room, Minnie nodded toward the food. "Don't insult her by letting that get cold."

Greg dutifully began to eat, savoring each mouthful.

"You say you're looking for Fiona," Minnie said a few minutes later.

"Yes."

"She returned to her home here. She inherited it when Jamie and Meggie died, of course, but at the time she wasn't ready to live there. I'm not certain why she chose to come back, but whatever the reason, I'm pleased to have her closer, even though she insists she hasn't been able to get settled in enough for a visit.'' She glanced at him slyly. ''Perhaps you can convince her otherwise.''

He smiled without responding.

''I'll have Becky give you directions. I hope you'll bring your client to visit with me someday soon. I would enjoy getting to know her.''

It was almost an hour later before he was able to get away from the two women who were filled with advice for him. As it turned out, Fiona's home was less than ten miles from Minnie's. When he pulled up in front of the house he could only stare around him in wonder.

The stone house stood on a promontory overlooking the loch. Rolling hills surrounded the area. The scene radiated serenity. The biggest difference between the area here and Glen Cairn was the thick foliage of the hills and the abundance of trees.

As soon as he stepped out of the car and opened the wooden gate, he heard a dog bark. McTavish had heard him. The bark was friendly and excited and Greg grinned. It sounded as if he would be welcomed by at least one resident of the house.

He followed the several steps up to a wide porch and walked to the front door, which had an oval pane of glass in it. He could see McTavish's feverish movements behind the door, but there was no other sign that someone was at home.

He knocked on the door and waited.

Although the hallway was shadowy, Greg could

see enough of the stairway that he knew when Fiona started down the steps, talking to McTavish.

Then, she opened the door and stared at him in shock. He, on the other hand, drank in her presence as a man in the desert might react to the sight of an oasis. All he wanted to do at the moment was grab her and clutch her to him and beg her never to disappear from his life.

"Greg?" she said faintly.

He nodded, not trusting his voice.

McTavish nosed past the door and greeted Greg in his own fashion. Greg turned to him with relief, needing a moment to get a grip on his emotions. "It's good to see you, too, fella," he said, rubbing McTavish's large head.

As though suddenly remembering her manners, Fiona said, "Please come in. You must be chilled standing out there." She held the door open while he and McTavish came inside.

"What a beautiful home you have," he said, looking around the wide foyer.

She smiled. "Thank you. It's much too large for one person. I've been trying to decide what I'm going to do with it."

"You'd sell it?" he asked in surprise.

"I'm not sure. My parents not only lived here, but my father had his office here, as well. I'm thinking about returning to school and finishing my medical studies. I could then use his office."

He looked into one of the front rooms, which

was furnished as a comfortable waiting room. "Is there somewhere we could talk?"

Without a word, she turned and led the way to the back of the hall. She opened a door and ushered him into a sitting room that held many of the items he'd become familiar with at the cottage.

"What made you decide to leave Glen Cairn?" he asked, looking around the room.

"It was time," she responded. When he didn't comment, she said, "I never expected to see you again. Why are you here?"

He turned and found her standing by the door as though ready to escape. She looked much too pale, and there were dark smudges beneath her eyes. He wanted to ask if she had been ill, but hesitated.

Fiona walked over to one of the chairs and sat, motioning him to do the same. The chair he chose was close to hers. He sat on the edge of the seat and leaned forward, his elbows on his knees.

"Are you all right?" he asked, unable to hide his concern.

Her face flushed, an endearing reminder of how easily she could be flustered. At least the color eased the earlier pale, pinched look.

"I'm a little tired," she admitted. "I've been busy getting unpacked and settled."

He took her hand, unable to resist touching her. "I'm sorry I left without saying goodbye. Leaving

you was one of the hardest things I've ever had
to do.''

Her expression lightened. ''You had a flight to
catch. I knew that.''

He took a deep breath and began to speak.

''My name is Gregory Alan Dumas. I've lived
in Queens my whole life. My mother died when I
was a kid and I lived with my alcoholic father until
I was old enough to take care of myself.''

Damn, this was even harder than he'd thought.

He cleared his throat. ''I decided I'd rather work
on the side of the law so I became a cop.'' He
paused…and took another deep breath.

''Eight years ago I met and married Jillian No-
reen Santini. We had a daughter. Three years ago
a slimeball whose accomplice was holding up a
convenience store accidentally killed Jill. I was off
duty at the time and we'd happened to be in the
store at the time the robbery began. Whether I was
off duty or not, I was a cop. I couldn't walk away
from a crime being committed, so I stayed and Jill
died.''

Greg heard the words—the objective explanation regarding Jill's death—without feeling the
acute pain of loss. For the first time since that time,
he acknowledged to himself that her death was a
tragic accident that he hadn't been able to prevent.
He'd responded to the robbery the way he was
trained to do. Given the same set of circumstances
he knew that he would make the same choices.

"I left the department after that and opened a private investigation firm."

He realized that he still held Fiona's hand. She hadn't taken her eyes off him since he began speaking.

"I'm sorry I didn't tell you all of this when you first asked me. At the time I was unaware of what was happening to me."

Fiona tugged her hand free and raised it to his cheek. "What was that?" she asked softly.

"I left my heart with you the morning I left, even though I wouldn't admit it to either of us at the time." He turned his head and kissed her palm. "You see, I didn't realize I'd fallen in love with you until you were no longer a part of my daily life."

He felt certain that his chest was going to burst as he struggled to get air into his lungs while his heart raced at an alarming rate.

"I know we never talked about what was happening between us, so I have no idea how you feel about any of this." He held both of her hands and discovered that her pulse was racing almost as fast as his.

He stopped speaking, wondering if anything he'd said had made any sense. None of it had been what he'd planned to say.

She lifted her hands to his shoulders and smiled. "The first night you were in my home, while your fever was raging, you thought I was Jill. You pulled me onto the bed and held me while you slipped your hand beneath my robe and gown. Until that night I'd never felt desire, never understood how powerful passion could be...even though I knew your words and actions were never meant for me.''

Greg stared at her in dismay. He vaguely recalled his fevered imaginings but nothing so—''I'm sorry, Fiona. I didn't know.''

She tightened her grip on his shoulders. ''Of course you didn't know and I would never have mentioned it if you hadn't returned. You see, you made me aware of you on a level I'd never known existed, much less experienced. I couldn't get you out of my mind after that.

''The last night you were here, I knew that I wanted all that passion to be directed at me, if only for that one night. I needed to experience lovemaking with you.'' She paused and with a shy smile, she added, ''I wasn't disappointed.''

Greg could no longer sit still. Without another word he scooped Fiona into his arms and strode to the hallway. After taking the stairs two at a time he paused in the upper hallway and said, ''Your room, Fiona,'' he said with impatience. ''Which one is it?''

She pointed to one of the doors that stood ajar. He continued down the hallway and pushed the slightly open door wider. Without a word he walked to the large bed. With frustrated eagerness, he quickly undressed them both before pulling back the covers and placing her under them.

As soon as he crawled in beside her she reached for him. Greg wrapped his arms around her and kissed her with all the pent-up love and passion that he had restrained downstairs. Without breaking the kiss, he rolled so that she was above him, her legs on either side of his hips. He touched her and knew she was ready for him. Without further hesitation he surged inside of her, taking her with a sense of possession that almost overwhelmed him.

He'd had some idea of taking her slowly, with gentleness, to express his love for her, but neither of them had the patience to prolong the moment. She rode him without pause until they both exploded into a mind-blowing climax.

Before they could slow their breathing, he was kissing her again—this time along her neck, creating a trail down her chest. There was no doubt in his mind who he was making love to and who he intended to love until the day he died.

With the first rush of urgency appeased, Greg took his time kissing and caressing her breasts. With a quick flip he had her on her back where he could love every inch of her body…a kiss at a time.

He lifted his head and looked at her as he slowly entered her.

When he pulled away slightly, they were both breathing hard.

"Marry me, Fiona," he managed to say while he moved in a lazy rhythm inside her. "Marry me or I'll be forced to keep you in bed until I can convince you we belong together."

She moved her hips upward to meet each of his thrusts, her sparkling gaze locked on his, revealing everything she felt for him. "I want to marry you," she managed to say, "but there's so much to consider—where we'll live, how your family will react to the…idea," she said with a moan of pleasure.

"We'll deal with all that. I promise," he replied, picking up the pace until they were too engrossed to speak.

Fiona peaked in a long, pulsating wave, tightening around him until he lost control and followed her.

He collapsed on the bed, his arms securely around Fiona, and drifted off to sleep.

Greg was awakened some time later to find Fiona attempting to move away from him. "Where you goin'?" he mumbled, holding her tighter.

"We need a fire," she said, nodding toward the embers in the fireplace of the bedroom.

"Give me a minute," he said, feeling as if his body had become melted wax.

She pulled away from him. "No. Stay there. I

won't be long.'' True to her word she was soon back in bed with him.

"So," he murmured, nibbling on her ear, "are you going to marry me? My family likes the idea. They hope that marriage will improve my disposition.''

She lifted her head to look down at him doubtfully. "You think?"

"Can't hurt. As you so kindly pointed out, there's lots of room for improvement.'' He stroked her back, edging her closer to him so that she was flush with him. "I'm looking into opening a branch of my office in Edinburgh. What do you think? Would that work for you?''

She caught her breath when he slid his hand around to her breast, toying with the nipple. "What about Tina and her grandparents?'' she managed to say.

"I think Minnie had a good idea. She suggested I move all of them over here.''

Fiona stiffened and pushed away from him so that she could see his face. "Minnie? Are you talking about *my* Aunt Minnie? When did she say that to you?''

"The morning after she and I sat up late talking while looking through photograph albums of you growing up.''

"You never told me about that!''

"I enjoyed the photographs. I'd told you I

wanted to see them. Minnie was kind enough to oblige my curiosity.''

''No, I'm talking about her suggestion that you move your family to Scotland.''

''Oh. Well, I guess this is my day for confessions.'' He looked at his watch. ''How would you like to return with me to Edinburgh tonight?''

''Tonight? Why?''

She looked so beautiful with the firelight glowing on her hair and body. He still wasn't used to the rush of love that swept over him whenever he looked at her.

Greg sat up and kissed the tip of her nose. ''There's someone there I want you to meet.''

* * * * *

We hope you enjoyed
MAN IN THE MIST,
Book I of Annette Broadrick's
new Special Edition series,
SECRET SISTERS.
Please look for the story of Kelly
and the man everyone thought was
TOO TOUGH TO TAME,
in Book II (SE #1581, 12/03) next
month.

For a sneak preview of
TOO TOUGH TO TAME,
turn the page...

Chapter One

September 2003

"**S**he's really gotten to you, hasn't she, Nick?"

Dominic Chakaris glanced over at Craig Bonner, his friend and vice president of Nick's extensive corporate holdings.

"Hell, no. The only reason I had her investigated was to find out why some woman I've never met had the gall to paint a portrait of me and publicly display it." Nick resumed staring at the view from his office high above the canyons of New York City, his hands in the pockets of his custom-made suit.

"Uh-huh," Craig replied.

Nick turned away from the view and walked to his desk. His cold gaze met Craig's as both men sat, Craig in front of Nick's massive desk, Nick sprawled in his chair. "What did our investigator find out?" Nick asked.

Craig had known Nick for more than ten years. He wasn't intimidated by the hawklike stare of his esteemed leader. He was probably the only one in Manhattan who could say that and not be lying through his teeth.

Okay, so he should have known Nick would deny that the artist and her portrait of him had been like a thorn in his foot, one that had festered since he'd learned of the painting's existence.

Being a diplomat by nature, Craig said no more. He glanced at the file in his hand and slid it across the desk to Nick, who flipped it open.

"According to our investigator's file," Craig said, "the artist's full name is Kelly Anne Mac-Leod, age twenty-four. Her parents are dead and she resides alone in the family home on Eighty-first Street. She majored in art history at Vassar. She spent her junior year in Italy and currently brings in a healthy amount of money for the portraits she paints. I understand there's a waiting list for the privilege of having her do a portrait." He lifted one shoulder and grinned. "See, I told you that you should be flattered."

Nick muttered something obscene—causing

Craig to laugh—and said, "Is this all you have?" He lifted the few sheets of paper and nodded at the photo attached to the inside cover of the file.

"There wasn't much to discover. She doesn't appear to be a stalker, which you should find immensely reassuring," Craig replied, enjoying Nick's discomfort. He was glad not to hear what Nick continued to mutter beneath his breath.

"Nothing here indicates why she chose to place my portrait on public display. Damn it, Craig, I don't care about her orphaned state or how much money she makes. From what I can see," he said, closing the file, "she appears to be like any other debutante, another pampered member of New York's elite." A class of people, Nick silently added, that he had little use for. "And I'm not flattered, as you very well know. Besides, the damned portrait is far from flattering."

Craig grinned. "Actually, it looks just like you."

Nick raised an eyebrow. "Is that right? The review of her show in the *Times* said that the portrait portrays me as hard and ruthless, a predator ready to pounce on some unsuspecting prey."

Craig grinned. "As I said, it looks just like you. Maybe I should take some candid photos of you at one of the board meetings and prove my point."

Nick stared balefully at his second-in-command and said, "Since you have little to add to this conversation, I've got work to do."

"I would imagine that what's really bothering you is the fact that Ms. MacLeod has accurately pegged you and you don't like it. She appears to know you quite well."

Nick shook his head. "That's impossible." He studied the photograph.

"I doubt that you could forget having met her." Craig stood and gave Nick a mock salute before he strolled out of the office.

Nick watched him close the door. He didn't like mysteries...and the reason behind the portrait of him was definitely a mystery. He'd received so many phone calls and comments about the damned thing that he'd gone to the gallery to see what the stir was about...and received the shock of his life.

There was no question that the painting was exceptionally well-done, but he couldn't fathom why he'd been chosen as its subject, or why the artist had portrayed him as she had.

There were no photographs of him that resembled the artist's vision. But the painting unnerved him—made him feel as if she'd invaded his privacy.

He focused on the photograph once again. She had pale blond hair and wore it pulled back from her face. Very few women could wear that austere style. Kelly was an exception.

Her intensely blue eyes stared into the camera with humor lurking in their depths. She had the beginnings of a smile curving her lips.

Looking closer, he realized that he had, in fact, seen her before.

He sat back in his chair, put his hands behind his head and recalled the night he'd first noticed her.

He avoided large social occasions as much as possible but in this case had felt obligated to go. One of his business associates had rented one of the city's largest ballrooms to honor his daughter for something. Maybe it was an engagement party.

Nick made it a point whenever he found it necessary to attend such a party to greet the people he knew and listen to any business gossip that reached his ear. Then, once he'd spoken to the host, he'd leave, thankful another painful duty had been fulfilled.

On that night he had paused in the doorway to look over the crowd, when he'd seen her. She was dancing, and the light from the chandeliers made her hair look like liquid gold. She'd worn it pulled back to the crown of her head where soft curls tumbled to her shoulders in studied disarray.

He'd looked to see if he knew her companion. He didn't. Then he'd searched for someone that he knew to ask who she was.

By the time he'd struck up a conversation with an acquaintance, the song had ended and she'd disappeared.

On his way out of the party a little later she had passed by him within a couple of feet, laughing at something said by one of the women she was with. He'd caught a hint of her light, floral perfume and saw that she was shorter than he'd first thought. Although she looked young, she exuded a self-confidence and grace that intrigued him.

Now he knew who she was. Her name was Kelly MacLeod.

He was intrigued to discover she was the artist who'd painted that damned portrait.

On impulse, Nick placed a call to the unlisted phone number his investigator had included. He waited through several rings before a sultry voice said, "Hi, this is Kelly. I can't interrupt the temperamental muse to take your call at the moment. Please leave your name, number and any message, and I'll get back to you as soon as I escape her clutches."

"This is Dominic Chakaris," he said after the beep. "I believe it's time we met in person."

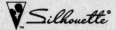

If you enjoyed what you just read,
then we've got an offer you can't resist!

Take 2 bestselling love stories FREE!
Plus get a FREE surprise gift!

✂

Your opinion is important to us! Please take a few moments to share your thoughts with us about your experiences with Harlequin and Silhouette books. Your comments will be very useful in ensuring that we deliver books you love to read. *Please take a few minutes to complete the questionnaire, then send it to us at the address below.*

Send your completed questionnaires to:
Harlequin/Silhouette Reader Survey, P.O. Box 9046, Buffalo, NY 14269-9046

1. As you may know, there are many different lines under the Harlequin and Silhouette brands. Each of the lines is listed below. Please check the box that most represents your reading habit for each line.

Line	Currently read this line	Do not read this line	Not sure if I read this line
Harlequin American Romance	❑	❑	❑
Harlequin Duets	❑	❑	❑
Harlequin Romance	❑	❑	❑
Harlequin Historicals	❑	❑	❑
Harlequin Superromance	❑	❑	❑
Harlequin Intrigue	❑	❑	❑
Harlequin Presents	❑	❑	❑
Harlequin Temptation	❑	❑	❑
Harlequin Blaze	❑	❑	❑
Silhouette Special Edition	❑	❑	❑
Silhouette Romance	❑	❑	❑
Silhouette Intimate Moments	❑	❑	❑
Silhouette Desire	❑	❑	❑

2. Which of the following best describes why you bought *this book?* One answer only, please.

the picture on the cover	❑	the title	❑
the author	❑	the line is one I read often	❑
part of a miniseries	❑	saw an ad in another book	❑
saw an ad in a magazine/newsletter	❑	a friend told me about it	❑
I borrowed/was given this book	❑	other: _____	❑

3. Where did you buy *this book?* One answer only, please.

at Barnes & Noble	❑	at a grocery store	❑
at Waldenbooks	❑	at a drugstore	❑
at Borders	❑	on eHarlequin.com Web site	❑
at another bookstore	❑	from another Web site	❑
at Wal-Mart	❑	Harlequin/Silhouette Reader	❑
at Target	❑	Service/through the mail	
at Kmart	❑	used books from anywhere	❑
at another department store or mass merchandiser	❑	I borrowed/was given this book	❑

4. On average, how many Harlequin and Silhouette books do you buy at one time?

I buy _____ books at one time	❑
I rarely buy a book	❑

MRQ403SSE-1A

5. How many times per month do you shop for any *Harlequin and/or Silhouette* books?
   One answer only, please.

1 or more times a week	❑	a few times per year	❑
1 to 3 times per month	❑	less often than once a year	❑
1 to 2 times every 3 months	❑	never	❑

6. When you think of your ideal heroine, which *one* statement describes her the best?
   One answer only, please.

She's a woman who is strong-willed	❑	She's a desirable woman	❑
She's a woman who is needed by others	❑	She's a powerful woman	❑
She's a woman who is taken care of	❑	She's a passionate woman	❑
She's an adventurous woman	❑	She's a sensitive woman	❑

7. The following statements describe types or genres of books that you may be
   interested in reading. Pick *up to 2 types* of books that you are most interested in.

I like to read about truly romantic relationships	❑
I like to read stories that are sexy romances	❑
I like to read romantic comedies	❑
I like to read a romantic mystery/suspense	❑
I like to read about romantic adventures	❑
I like to read romance stories that involve family	❑
I like to read about a romance in times or places that I have never seen	❑
Other: _____	❑

*The following questions help us to group your answers with those readers who are
similar to you. Your answers will remain confidential.*

8. Please record your year of birth below.

   19 _____

9. What is your marital status?

   single ❑   married ❑   common-law ❑   widowed ❑
   divorced/separated ❑

10. Do you have children 18 years of age or younger currently living at home?

    yes ❑   no ❑

11. Which of the following best describes your employment status?

    employed full-time or part-time ❑   homemaker ❑   student ❑
    retired ❑   unemployed ❑

12. Do you have access to the Internet from either home or work?

    yes ❑   no ❑

13. Have you ever visited eHarlequin.com?

    yes ❑   no ❑

14. What state do you live in?

    _____

15. Are you a member of Harlequin/Silhouette Reader Service?

    yes ❑   Account # _____   no ❑   MRQ403SSE-1B

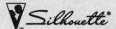
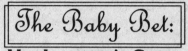

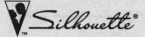

COMING NEXT MONTH

SSECNM1103